SHE'S GIVEN HER HEART AWAY

"I feel like I'm going to die if I don't have him. I want to *own* him. I want to pick him up in my arms and go running down the street with him and tuck him into my tool kit," Sibella said desperately. "I love him so much I wish we could *explode* together. That our atoms and electrons could get *inside* each other. I'm so sad. I love him so much, I'm sad, that's how special he is."

"Profoundly moving and humorous, a story that may be judged the best of his award winners."
—*Publishers Weekly*

"Fast paced with natural dialogue and appealingly eccentric characters."
—*Booklist*

"What is new and compelling is the force with which Sibella's pain is delineated....Her misery and her refusal to be done in by that misery will communicate to kids and haunt adults."
—*Voice of Youth Advocates*

Bantam Books by Paul Zindel
Ask your bookseller for the books you have missed

CONFESSIONS OF A TEENAGE BABOON
THE EFFECT OF GAMMA RAYS ON
  MAN-IN-THE-MOON MARIGOLDS
THE GIRL WHO WANTED A BOY
I NEVER LOVED YOUR MIND
MY DARLING, MY HAMBURGER
PARDON ME, YOU'RE STEPPING ON MY
  EYEBALL!
THE PIGMAN
THE PIGMAN'S LEGACY
A STAR FOR THE LATECOMER
  (with Bonnie Zindel)
THE UNDERTAKER'S GONE BANANAS

THE GIRL
WHO
WANTED
A BOY

Paul Zindel

BANTAM BOOKS
TORONTO · NEW YORK · LONDON · SYDNEY

To Marybeth and Eddie

This low-priced Bantam Book
has been completely reset in a type face
designed for easy reading, and was printed
from new plates. It contains the complete
text of the original hard-cover edition.
NOT ONE WORD HAS BEEN OMITTED.

RL 6, IL age 12 and up

THE GIRL WHO WANTED A BOY
A Bantam Book / published by arrangement with
Harper & Row, Publishers, Inc.

PRINTING HISTORY
Harper & Row edition published July 1981
Bantam edition / September 1982

The excerpt on page 41 from "I'm a Yandee Doodle Dandy"
© *Copyright: Edward B. Marks Music Corporation. Used by*
permission.

The line on page 44 from "Laughing on the Outside, Crying
on the Inside" © *1946 BROADCAST MUSIC INC. Copyright*
Renewed and Assigned to WARNER-TAMERLANE PUBLISHING
CORP. All Rights Reserved. Used by permission.

ISBN 0-553-22540-5

Published simultaneously in the United States and Canada

Bantam Books are published by Bantam Books, Inc. Its trade-
mark, consisting of the words "Bantam Books" and the por-
trayal of a rooster, is Registered in U.S. Patent and Trademark
Office and in other countries. Marca Registrada. Bantam
Books, Inc., 666 Fifth Avenue, New York, New York 10103.

1

As Sibella Cametta sloshed along home from school, her eyes were drawn to a boy with red hair making a snowball. *Cute*, she thought, *but definitely not magic*. Her boots plowed through the slush as she moved farther down the street. There, another boy!—but he looked a bit like an anteater. She'd need someone more civilized, someone who could appreciate her simple, ordinary existence.

She yanked her load of books higher on her hip and turned into Treadwell Avenue—in the homestretch at last. It was getting so dark so early. The coldest December she could remember, and it seemed every house had a snowman staring at her. She watched the wind-pushed snow dust over their cold bodies—carrots, pieces of coal, absolutely absurd specks to portray eyes and noses and mouths. Just one more lineup of subzero males who didn't even know she was alive. *A clod, that's what I am, a bounding clod—fifty pounds of science books. The cheap artificial fur coat, a shapeless cardigan peeking out, and my stupid jumper.* If there was a boy looking down from an attic window, he was probably horrified. If a boy came out of a door somewhere or was driving by in a car, how silly she must look, how insignificant! *How eccentric!* she moaned to herself. *A penguin, that's what I am,* she thought, going up the steps of the small wood-framed house with the postage-stamp front yard. *I'm a penguin.*

Sibella went straight to her room. Off came the phony fur, the unforgivable cardigan. She put her books on her desk, kicked her boots toward the radiator, and plopped smack across the bed, pen in hand. She had so much to tell as she yanked her diary out of the bedstand drawer. "Oh, my dear diary, here it is almost Christmas and I still haven't found a boy...and what's even worse, I'm tired of bellyaching about it." She decided to pad the page with a description of an experiment they did that afternoon in chem class, during which Mr. Herbert got his eyebrows blown off. He looked so funny with that instant sunburn, which made him look like his face had spent two weeks in Acapulco but had forgotten to take his neck with it. Her eyes drifted along her bookshelf and stopped on her sister Maureen's yearbook—the only book her sister had bequeathed her besides a very worn copy of *How to Pick Up Boys.* Lucky Maureen, gorgeous, terrific—*everything I'm not*—and out of school to boot. She got down the yearbook. There were so many boys who had signed it. "To Maureen, You are a real crazy girl, and neat too. Never change, because that's just the way I love you. Joey." There was another graduation photo of a boy who looked like a very interesting person except for his very pointed chin. "Dear Maureen, You've always been a real close friend, and I will never forget all the good times we had together. You'll make a hell of a Comptometer operator. With love, your friend, Goose." A whole yearbook full of boys saying how much they loved her sister! Sibella sighed again. *I'll be lucky if I can get my chemistry teacher to sign my yearbook: "Dear Sibella, what a wonderful test tube you've been. With great respect, Mr. Herbert." Or my physics teacher: "Dear Sibella, you excelled in pulley systems. I'll never forget all the fun you were with Newton's laws. Yours truly, Mr. Brightenbach."* Not one sensational boy would sign her book.

Sibella got up from the bed and moved to the workshop section of her room. The hammers, pliers, screwdrivers, tape measure, incline plane, saws, cements—everything neat as a pin. She retrieved her bankbooks from behind the huge Johnson's auto repair manual. She had $2,420.70 in Chase and $1,108.63 in Citibank. She'd only opened the account at Chase because they had offered a nifty set of wrenches. Well, at least she was getting richer, she comforted herself. In the loot department she really wasn't doing too bad for a high school sophomore. In another month there would be more interest to add on, and there were always a lot of jobs waiting for her. Mr. Hertzberg at the drugstore had asked her to lay some tiles by a sliding door. Mrs. Russo across the street wanted her to make a built-in bookcase. Hendrick's TV store begged her to do more freelancing on stereo and TV repairs. In fact, during the last year word of mouth that she could do automotive, carpentry, electronic, and mechanical repair had spread like wildfire. All right, so maybe it was a little unusual. Maybe she was the only girl she knew whose ambition was to grow up to own and operate a Mobile gas station. But it was paying off. Or was it? Money, money, money, oh what good was it all without a boy?

She heard her mother's door open at the end of the hall, but those weren't her mother's footsteps coming out. The noises went down the stairs to the kitchen. Sibella decided to check it out.

From the bottom of the stairs she could see straight through to the back of the house. A strange man dressed in a shiny shirt curving over his beer belly and shimmering pants was digging through the refrigerator. He looked like a fired Fred Astaire dance instructor. Forty years old, she decided, and a big nose. The man turned, suddenly spying Sibella standing in the kitchen doorway.

"Hi," he said.

She saw his eyes lingering on her hair. She just knew he was thinking it looked like blond linguine.

"Who are you?" she asked.

"Charlie." He smiled. "And you must be Sibella."

"Mom's already told you about me, I see."

"She said you were a good daughter."

"Are you her new *friend*?"

"I'd like to be your mother's friend," Charlie said. "I'd like to be your friend too." Charlie took a container of skim milk from the refrigerator,

4

shut the door, and walked to the sink. "Your mother's a very wonderful woman," Charlie started.

Sibella decided not to listen to another word. She turned quickly, and zipped back down the hall and upstairs. She'd have to let this one know where he stood. Nobody was going to play Poppa to her. Her father was still alive and well and working at a chemical firm in Manhattan—and living with Pauline, that nice old secretary who used to smoke cigarettes and let the fumes curl up into her nose and then back out her mouth before she gave up smoking all together. No, she wouldn't be listening to any worn-out dance instructors or used-car salesmen or any of the other boyfriends her mother brought home.

Back in her room she looked at the photo of her father on the dresser. He was standing in front of a huge oil refinery, smiling and waving in a lab smock. She went over and looked at her second-favorite photo lying next to it. Her father, smiling, waving as usual, with her, two years old, sitting in a go-cart her father had just built. "Take a little girl through your window," she began to sing to herself. "Take a little girl through your window." That was her favorite song her father used to sing to her.

She'd get out now, that's what she'd do. Just go and have a good time. Today at school was hard enough. Back on went the sweater. On went the phony fur, gloves, scarf. Anything to avoid the cocktail hour with her mother and latest heartthrob. She grabbed one of her physics books and her sister's copy of *How to Pick Up Boys*. She'd go read those in the library if she got bored. Her tool kit, she'd take that just in case. Actually, if she worked fast she could make twenty dollars before dinner doing odd jobs, so the day wouldn't be a total waste.

She sailed down the stairs and out of the house. The sky was dark blue with little snow clouds hovering far off in Jersey. Her tool kit banged at her side as she plodded back down the street. *Plop! Squish! Squash!*

She decided she needed a hot chocolate, so she went straight to Steckman's, the soda shop where everybody who was anybody went after school. The best-looking boys and girls always sat in booths closest to the jukebox. There were only eight booths and about twenty tables. If you had a booth, everyone looked at you. Of course, if you were a social cripple, you sat at the counter. That was okay only if you were a freshman, and then if you were really *untouchable*, you simply walked in and bought a chocolate lollipop at the cash register.

Sibella sat at the counter and ordered a hot chocolate. While she sipped she made believe she was checking her screw inventory in the toolbox. After she had counted almost every screw, she decided to open her physics book and read about the filaments in cathode tubes. She really felt she was somewhat limited in physics, and the only chance she had of understanding electron flow was to constantly think of electricity as being a stream of water. It would work for high school physics, but electrons were not really drops of water, and unless her mind made some tremendous

6

breakthrough, she knew that running a Mobil gas station was a more realistic goal than heading up something like the laboratory at the Mount Palomar Observatory.

Mr. Steckman, the gray-haired owner, came over. "How are you doing, Sibella?"

"Okay," Sibella said nervously. What she liked about Mr. Steckman was he always seemed to understand her. What's more, she felt he really *appreciated* her.

"How's life treating you?" he wanted to know.

"Pretty good," she said.

"Good." He smiled. "Say, I need a couple of fluorescent lights put in over the front counter. You think you can get to it next week?"

"Sure," Sibella said. "I'll come in and look it over. Maybe I can do the work next Sunday, if you let me in."

"Thanks, Sibella," Mr. Steckman said.

"Thank *you*."

Sibella clutched her tool kit and surveyed the area where the lights would go. Now that she had something to really think about, she was able to do what she had really come in there to do in the first place. Slowly she let her eyes drift toward the jukebox area. Some record was playing, with a girl moaning about love gone wrong. There was one boy, his hand raised, clutching a Coke. His face looked a little like rubber, trying so hard to entertain. *Too much of a fool, but nice hair.* And another boy literally jumping up and down in the aisle. He had a nice laugh, but what a goofball. Then she focused on Doug Rogow—from her phys-

7

ics class—with long brown hair, his ears peeking out from under it. He was nice-looking, a little like a Russian folk dancer. But there was also something about him that looked a little like a washwoman, a very masculine washwoman who should be scrubbing floors.

And then there were the *awful* girls. One dressed in overalls pretending to be an innocent farmer's daughter. And another one with short bangs and straight hair, and a chin like a wrestler. And the *awful* Mary Anne Beckly, with wet little ringlets hanging around her face and big brown eyes. She was doing gurgling things with a straw. And the real horrors, the gorgeous cheerleaders—their terrific gray-and-white-trimmed jackets with little pins and letters on them. A pack of really pretty, healthy girls who looked like they were weaned on carrots, hanging, literally hanging on the football players. But her mother had always told her not to worry about beautiful cheerleaders. All beautiful cheerleaders grow up to be very ugly old maids who push supermarket baskets around, and their legs get as wide as elephants'. Sibella knew it wasn't true, but it was a great theory.

She looked back at the ceiling as though checking the electrical accesses for the forthcoming installation, and then she let her eyes switch back to the specific focus on the boys.

One boy near the jukebox had nice socks, big high white ones with stripes around them, clean to the calves, and he was wearing shorts in December. Now *that* was cute. He probably also slept with a blue organdy canopy over his bed. Then there was Jack Kayhill, a boy from her lunch period who played in the band, very interesting lips and nice posture. And there they were—seven football guys lined up in a double booth, big numbers on their chests. Physically they did look delicious. And they all had shoulders, big strong shoulders. But while there was something excitingly masculine about them, she never once got the impression any one of them could be tender. She felt they'd much prefer a good medium-rare steak to a kiss.

But there were some other girls with boys who looked just nice. Some she knew from around school. They looked like nice happy couples, sipping their sodas and talking normally. That's what she wanted, just to be able to sit with a boy and talk. But it would have to be a boy she felt something for. Someone who when she looked at him would make her think only how much she loved him. Love would be waiting for her somewhere, and she knew when she saw *that* boy, she would know it. When she saw the boy meant for her, there would be a circus in her heart—no, in her mind. It would be a mind circus. *Somewhere there was a boy who would give her a mind circus.*

2

The next morning Sibella stumbled her way to school. It was only three blocks from her door to the entrance of Port Richmond High School, but it seemed like an eight-mile death march with 1,500 oppressed fellow-pubescent prisoners. All the kids just plodded along both sides of the street. Occasionally a teacher's car would go by. She recognized Mrs. Mills, who taught English—the only English teacher she had ever heard of who had a doctorate in Shakespearean studies and was so brilliant nobody ever knew what she was talking about. Then she glimpsed the Spanish teacher, who thought he was a flamenco dancer and the answer to every girl's dream. And of course there was Mrs. Wilmont, whom she had absolutely adored when she had taken a biology course with her. She had never forgotten about the time Mrs. Wilmont told her she had found a baby chipmunk that would have frozen to death if she hadn't kept it warm by nestling it down the front of her dress. The class was stunned when Mrs. Wilmont confided in them that one time the postman had rung the bell to deliver a package, and she opened the door forgetting about the chipmunk; and as the postman was talking to her the chipmunk climbed up out of her bosom.

Actually, on the whole, Port Richmond had some terrific teachers, really down-to-earth. And Sibella imagined quite a few of them were old maids who were probably as lonely as she was. Nowadays she knew you didn't have to be a woman to end up as an old maid, and some of the single teachers seemed to really *like* living alone. "Independent," they called it. Maybe someday that would sound good to her, but now in her life she wanted a boy.

She had physics first period with Mr. Brightenbach, a very sweet man who often inspired her. But it was much too early today to be inspired. "Magnetism," Mr. Brightenbach was telling the class of thirty-eight kids, "has been known about for centuries. There were early legends concerning its discovery. One of these, found in a Greek manuscript written before the birth of Christ, tells about the wonders performed by a roving band of iron workers called Cabiri. One of their astounding feats was to cause an ironlike stone, now known as lodestone, to attract and hold several iron rings. . . ."

That is about all she could remember hearing before she was aware of the laughter. The class was laughing, Mr. Brightenbach was staring at her. She knew she had dozed off. She so hoped she hadn't snored.

"What's going on?" Mr. Brightenbach wanted

to know. "I realize I'm boring, but you don't usually fall asleep, Sibella. Are you stoned?"

"No, Mr. Brightenbach."

She saw his hand reaching out to her desk. Oh my God, he had *the book*. He had seen *the book*. It was in his hands.

"You were reading *this*, Sibella?" Mr. Brightenbach asked. "You were reading *How to Pick Up Boys*?"

The class screamed with laughter. Sibella could feel her face going scarlet. Even Mr. Brightenbach's face was red. She could tell in his eyes he was sorry he had mentioned the title of the book. He just quickly put the book down on her desk and walked back to the front of the class.

"If you're doing a report for psychology or some special English project, please don't do it during my class. You're all going to have enough problems with understanding why metals attract each other."

Sibella felt like dying. Maybe she could induce cardiac arrest and just keel over and let it all end right there. She slipped *How to Pick Up Boys* into her shoulder bag, and just hung her head like an ostrich waiting for it all to go away, waiting for the danger to move on.

"Now one thing that we do know is that the lodestone of the Cabiri was a natural magnet," Mr. Brightenbach went on, "which magnetized the rings and thus held them together by an invisible force...." She was grateful the class had returned to the boredom of magnetism. After physics there was math, and then gym with the tough Miss Hammel, who looked like she could play for the Pittsburgh Steelers; and lunch supervised by the sweet Miss Gail, whom kids used to always throw pennies and M&Ms at; and then came a few of the electives. There always seemed to be nicer boys in electives.

There was a boy who sat next to her named Ziegler in Miss Broom's music class. He used to make animal noises while Miss Broom would talk about the beauty of Chopin. Sometimes he'd work the whole class up into such a wild frenzy, Miss Broom, who was about 173 years old, would snatch off her eyeglasses and begin to suck on the frame. When she felt everything was really going bananas, she'd rush to the piano and begin to play "Dry Bones" in jazz tempo. She was obviously as mad as a hatter, but banging out "Dem bones, dem bones, dem dry bones" seemed to quiet down the pack of teenage coyotes she used to get for every class.

The rest of the day would become just little images for her diary: some boy walking down the hall with a pompom; another boy with long blond hair wearing stripes like he had just gotten out of reform school. She walked by the principal's office and there was another boy in there who looked like he was about to be sent to the electric chair. And there was a despondent couple in one stairwell who looked like they were falling *out* of love.

Finally in art she got a chance to really get into her new book. She felt as though the writer was writing directly on her heart: *When it gets right down to basics*, the book said, *onto the bus steps an*

13

incredible-looking boy, a delectable-looking boy. He looks warm, sweet, special. His pants are sexy yet tasteful. His deep, dark eyes are soulful, his lips sensuous. Immediately you have visions of intimate encounters, wines by candlelight, hugging and making love. You want to call over to him. You want to say, "Here, boy, sit right here next to me." Well, this book is going to tell you how to get that boy not only to sit next to you but to smother you with love and tender kisses.

Sibella felt her entire body sigh. She sighed all the way home from school. She sighed sloshing back out with her tool kit and delivering the lamp she had fixed for Mr. Wise, and the Plexiglas picture frame she had glued for Mrs. Blizinsky. And she sighed, especially, when sitting down for dinner with her mother and Charlie.

Mrs. Cametta scooped string beans onto Charlie's plate as though she had selected each one personally and painted it with butter. There was no question that she was a rather pretty woman for forty-eight. Admirable, Sibella often thought. She thought her mother had very admirable features, well-cut bangs and kind of straight hair in a bob as though she was living in 1920. Only one dangerous feature—her large ears. When it came to nose, mouth, and eyes, her mother was as pretty as anybody she'd ever seen. Oh, it really wasn't surprising to her that her sweet father had once married her, and that now many men were still interested in her.

Charlie had on another shiny shirt. His nose had gotten bigger; his hair was slicked back now and he had turned out to be a used-car salesman.

He said he was one of the top dynamic influences at Casa de Volvo, but Sibella seriously doubted that.

"How was school today, Sibella?" Mrs. Cametta asked.

Sibella was chewing a mouthful of veal parmigiana and wasn't about to start chatting.

"*I* loved school," Charlie offered. "Of course I didn't have as many science classes as you have. I never met a girl who had so many science courses."

Sibella wanted to burp. She decided she'd better not. She forced herself to look at this used-car salesman with the mozzarella getting entwined in his teeth. Now it seemed like her mother *and* Charlie weren't going to stop staring at her until she made some sort of sound, but she wouldn't.

Her mother finally said, "Mrs. Blizinsky called about the picture frame. Said you did a marvelous job on it—that you had it in some kind of clamp."

"I had it in a vise."

"There you go, correcting me again," Mrs. Cametta pointed out. "I just think you're so weird, Sibella. Don't you feel weird with all those galvanometers and pliers? I never knew a girl who went from dolls straight to pliers. You should be getting involved in more social activities. *Boys!* Don't you ever think about *boys?*"

"Your mother's right, Sibella," Charlie said. "If you saw my son Rocky you'd start wearing a dress. I tell you, by your age, we were really doing some hot stuff, and..."

Mrs. Cametta glanced at Charlie, shooting him a look that made his words freeze in his throat.

15

Sibella always enjoyed watching her mother control her men. In fact one of the ground rules of her mother's having a man in the house was that it had to be someone she could run like a puppet. Someone totally unlike Sibella's father. Sibella's dad was his own man, that was one thing for sure!

Sibella just went about the business of eating and let her mother and Charlie talk about a variety of subjects, from the truly destructive qualities of rock music to the retail value of used Volvos. Sibella thanked God there was a newspaper lying on the table near the glass lily-shaped vase with phony dogwood hanging out of it. The newspaper was open to the sports page. *Charlie must like sports, a real man,* she thought. *Just loves to sit on his butt and cheer while other people are really getting out and doing things.* Her eye caught headlines that did not fascinate her, like "Yanks Win—Stay Half Game Ahead" or "Now Big Louie Can Concentrate on Batting Average." And a more daring peg: "One Coach's Purgatory." Really, what an exaggeration. If somebody wanted to know about hell, they could just ask her.

She started reading the ads for the health clubs where men and women were supposed to frolic together using Nautilus weight-lifting equipment. And there were horrible items about guns, and the latest shooting techniques. How to make a fishing fly to catch wide pike. She was about to let out another big sigh when she spotted a picture of a couple of young boys standing next to a little

16

race car. The headline was "Midget Raceway Opens in Mariner's Harbor." Mariner's Harbor was right next to Port Richmond, so she'd seen the huge field when they were paving it and putting in the twisting cement roadway and building the little grandstand. At first she'd thought it was going to be a water slide. Now in the picture it had opened, and there were all these kids going there to lay down their cash so they could get into these midget race cars and make believe they were in the Indianapolis 500. But what caught her attention was one face in particular. The captain didn't say anything about him. He looked like a mechanic, somebody who was in charge of the cars. He had an incredible smile, a bright-eyed innocence, as though it was the first time his picture was ever taken. And there was something about his thin legs and long arms, and the way the words "Mariner's Midgets" hung down his chest. He looked like *fun*. He was handsome, had brown hair—maybe it was supposed to be blond, but it looked dark in the newspaper reproduction. He looked friendly, special. He was better than any movie star she had ever seen. Yes, *his eyes are soulful, his lips sensuous*. He looked like he was a boy of the world, and he couldn't be more than eighteen. He looked like he knew all about law, and medicine, and photography, and the theater. He looked like someone who was really going places, maybe a doctor-to-be or a journalist. But it didn't matter; there was something about this boy that was leaping out of the newspaper, machine-gunning

17

Sibella Cametta from the sports page of the *Staten Island Advance*. A machine gun screaming, *"I am fun and romance."*

"What's the matter, Sibella?" she heard her mother say.

"Oh, nothing," Sibella said. She was fighting a distinct desire to lift the sports page up to her lips and start kissing the photo of this unknown mechanic. She wanted to dive into the newspaper. She wanted to cut the picture out, tear it out, and wear it on her heart. Mariner's Midgets became a poem.

"Excuse me, Mother," Sibella said. "I have a little indigestion. I'm going to need an Alka-Seltzer."

"Of course, dear," Mrs. Cametta agreed.

"Gas is really terrible," Charlie sympathized.

Sibella got up gently from the table.

"Are you finished with the newspaper?" she asked.

"Oh, sure," Charlie aaid.

"Thank you." Sibella picked up the paper as though it was a priceless Dead Sea Scroll. She tried not to appear excited as she moved out of the dining room and started up the stairs. As she neared her room she picked up speed. She flung the door open, slammed it shut, leaped across the bed, and spread the picture out again. She ripped her diary off the bookcase, and she began to write frantically and passionately, "Dear Diary, On this day I have found *the boy*."

3

The ad was on the entertainment page: "Mariner's Harbor Midget Raceway. Let us put you in the seat of your own Grand Prix racer." There was a giant drawing of a race car with oversized tires. The kid sitting in the seat looked like a midget, and the hood looked about fifty feet larger than the kid. "For the thrill of a lifetime! 555-6190. Open Fridays, Saturdays, and Sundays." That was par for Staten Island. It seemed like the Island closed down except for weekends. But here it was only Tuesday. Maybe *someone* would be there anyway.

She hesitated, then grabbed the phone and began to dial. A recording answered, "Thank you for calling Mariner's Harbor Midget Raceway. We're open Fridays, Saturdays, and Sundays from nine A.M. to midnight. Five laps are a dollar sixty per lap. Ten laps are one twenty-five per lap. Twenty-lap special, one dollar per lap. Thank you for calling Mariner's Harbor Midget Raceway. Come on down and have your dream come true."

Sibella dialed the number again. She knew, absolutely knew, the voice belonged to *him*. It was the most beautiful voice she had ever heard from any boy. He sounded so *realistic*. So down-to-earth. Obviously uncomfortable with the job of making the recording. There was probably some old cranky boss who owned the whole thing and knew it was better to have some young boy's voice do the recording. This was the perfect voice. "Twenty-lap special, one dollar per lap." He did it so convincingly, so *enticingly*.

She was about to dial the number again when a shriek reverberated from the downstairs hallway. She knew instantly her sister had landed.

Sibella went out to the hall and looked downstairs. She could see Maureen whirling around, taking off her scarf and coat. It annoyed her the way Maureen's hair was able to cascade and bounce even in a snowstorm. Maureen, nineteen years old—and everyone, just everyone, said she looked just like Marilyn Monroe. She had turned out to be one of the most glamorous Comptometer operators in the world, which, Sibella knew, meant she was nothing but a keypunch operator and probably as inept at that as she was at everything in high school except making out.

Maureen looked up, caught Sibella. "Bessie," she screamed, "*Bessie*, how's my *little Bessie*?"

Sibella loathed it when Maureen called her Bessie. Just because Sibella had agreed at the age of six to play the back of a cow called Bessie in her kindergarten play, there was no reason to keep that horrible name going. Maureen had said over the years she was only being kind because she couldn't bear the fact that her poor kid sister was stuck with a real name like Sibella.

"Chucky," Maureen yelled, "you've just got to meet my little sister."

Sibella descended farther and got a good look at Chucky. Chucky looked very big and rugged, but mentally he didn't look like he was pulling a full train. He had a peaches-and-cream complexion, just like Maureen, and Sibella could picture ·the two of them running along beaches in white scanty bathing suits showing off their legs. Chucky's black hair looked like someone from Walton's Mountain had clapped a bowl on his head and done a fast shear around the edges. What was most unbearable was that Maureen was practically doing a dance in her high heels. How anyone could survive wearing high heels in two feet of snow was beyond her.

"So how's tricks?" Maureen bubbled. She grabbed Sibella and began to dance around with her, giving her a big hug and a kiss on each cheek which made her cascading hair slap Sibella's ears. Maureen was a shocking contrast to Sibella, oozing personality, extroverted, gorgeous, sexy, aggressive. She had been voted the best all-around body in high school. And she knew more than anyone that she had graduated only because she could do a rather exemplary baton act.

"This is Chucky. Isn't he just a *dream*?" Maureen insisted on knowing.

"Very nice to meet you, Chucky," Sibella said somberly.

Sibella was expecting him to say, "Oh, my God,

Maureen, she doesn't look anything like you. She looks like a nun." Instead he flashed a big smile. "Nice to meet you, Bessie," he said.

By now Mrs. Cametta and Charlie had made it into the hallway, and there was so much noise, Sibella became frightened that the cops might be called out. Much too much kissing and hugging, Sibella thought. She couldn't bear the way Maureen was making it clear it was *Oh, such a pleasure* to meet Charlie. *Oh, such a pleasure* that her mother had a new friend. In seconds Mrs. Cametta had corralled them all around the table and was pouring coffee. Maureen never stopped laughing or talking about all the things she and Chucky were doing together—the movies, the concert, picnics on ice floes, ice-skating! No magical experience was escaping their new relationship. Maureen would take a sip of coffee and then do a run around with a lipstick, which made her lips look mirrored.

"Why, I think it would be wonderful to have you stay with us," Mrs. Cametta managed to summarize from the laughter out of Maureen and the grunting from Chucky. "You can have your old room and Chucky can sleep on the couch down here."

"Oh, no, mother." Maureen laughed. "You don't understand. We're *living* together."

Sibella watched her mother for her reaction. Mrs. Cametta paused, then smiled graciously.

"Oh, of course," Mrs. Cametta said. "Then you can both stay together in your old room. Will you be getting married?"

Maureen and Chucky laughed so hard at that one, even Mrs. Cametta winced.

Maureen sat upright. "No, you don't understand, Mom. I don't love him *that* much. He's more or less a comfort, aren't you, Chucky?"

"Yes, just a comfort." Chucky laughed.

"How long have you been comforting each other?" Sibella asked.

Maureen screamed. "Isn't she a delight? Isn't she just a delight, Chucky? Did you see? I told you she was funny. She's hilarious."

Charlie looked as though he didn't know what on earth was going on, and just kept reaching out to grab very large pieces of Sara Lee coffee cake. The crumbs rolled down his shimmering shirt like water hitting oil.

"Say something *else* funny," Maureen insited. "I told Chucky what a card you were. What a priceless card."

Sibella squirmed as everyone looked at her. She cleared her throat, but even then they kept looking. So finally she said it.

"Chucky is short for Charles, isn't it?" Sibella asked.

"Yes," Chucky admitted.

"Well, isn't that nice," Sibella pointed out. "Now Mom and Maureen *both* have Charlies."

Maureen screamed so loudly this time Sibella thought glassware would shatter. In fact they were all laughing, and ordinarily she would have felt terrible. Lonesome, terrible, and sad. But she wasn't even in the room with them. She really wasn't even talking to them. Her mind was on another wavelength which was speeding around curves and corners, and there were clowns beginning to put on makeup. A calliope was playing somewhere in the distance. Someone was climbing a trapeze rope, getting ready to swing. Somewhere in her mind she could hear a circus warming up.

Dear Diary, she wrote that night. *I have fallen in love with a boy in the sports section. We haven't met yet, but when we do, I believe with all my heart that our two solitudes will protect and touch and meet each other....*

4

Sibella heard the music pounding through the floor of her room. Her eyes had barely opened from a dream about playing miniature golf with a dwarf, when she was reminded that Maureen had come home with her latest live-in to lounge around while their Greenwich Village apartment was being scraped and painted. She tried crawling back under the comforter, but that only emphasized the music. It was so forceful it made her toes shake.

She got her act together, brushed her teeth, went downstairs. There was Maureen twirling, jumping, dipping, shaking, *cascading*—all of which was supposed to be known as dancing for Chucky. Chucky was still in pajamas, his huge legs swung over the arms of a chair, his lips pushing smoke rings of grass up into the air. He was clapping. "Go, Mo! Shake it, Mo!"

It looked like Maureen was going to totally fly up into the air. Either that or drill a hole in the floor. A helicopter, Sibella thought. My sister is a blond helicopter.

"Good morning, Bessie," Maureen called out.

25

Her voice took on a sort of Doppler effect from her motions.

Chucky just sort of scratched himself and smiled as his greeting.

"GOOD MORNING," Sibella deliberately screamed at the top of her lungs, startling her sister and Chucky. She stuck her fingers into her ears and plodded straight through the living room into the kitchen, slamming the door. There was sort of a swishing sound near her and she realized her mother was up and about.

"Sibella, I really think it's about time you and I had a talk," Mrs. Cametta said.

"You know how I love to chat, Mom," Sibella said, grabbing for the orange juice and swigging it down.

Mrs. Cametta moved quickly to set up a spot for Sibella at the table. She was parading as though deliberately showing off a new Sears, Roebuck quilted bathrobe, and what appeared to be some sort of pearls around her neck. *Well, she's dressing for the man she loves*, Sibella said to herself.

"How's Charlie this morning?"

"Fine," Mrs. Cametta said.

"Good. What do you want to talk to me about?"

"Nothing," Mrs. Cametta started, "nothing *much*. I was just wondering if you were all right."

"What do you mean by 'all right'?"

"I mean your head. Does you head feel all right?"

"Yes, Mom. Why do you ask?"

"Because you're acting weirder than usual. I think your emotions are showing too much."

"How can my emotions show too much?"

"Well, you looked so angry last night," Mrs. Cametta reminded her. "Are you disturbed because Maureen and I have Charlies, or is it because Maureen's boyfriend is going to stay with her in her room? Is that what's disturbing you?"

"No," Sibella said. "I don't care what anyone else does as long as they don't do it in the street and frighten the horses."

"Would you like an English muffin with Parkay squirted into it and a slab of cheese?"

"Thanks, Mom."

"I think the problem is that you're becoming inconsiderate," Mrs. Cametta elaborated, going to the toaster oven and ripping apart a muffin. "It's like you resent the fact that I date. You can't seem to bear that people dance, that people sing, that people hold on to each other *tenderly* in this world. Chucky even pointed it out, and he just met you. I told him that you never had a boyfriend and that you're just jealous."

"You didn't, Mom, tell me you didn't."

"All right, I didn't, but I thought that would get your attention. What I did tell him was that ever since I can remember, all you've had was electromagnets on the brain. Darling, boys don't want to caress an electromagnet."

"Look, Mom, I think there's a big difference between being an electromagnet and lassoing every used-car salesman who comes along."

"Charlie is going to own his own distributorship—BMW. He's going all the way to BMW. Honey, what I'm trying to tell you is you're the one who's uptight, not me."

Sibella took another slug of orange juice and started eating a tablespoon of butter.

"You're going to have to get with it, kid," Mrs. Cametta continued. "You'd better start painting your lips and putting on some mascara or move to Fiji. I think only the men wear makeup in Fiji. Honey, I try to set an example for you. I wanted you to see that human beings can be affectionate to each other."

"Oh, you set some example, Mom," Sibella mumbled. "I remember you with that bus driver right here in the kitchen."

"He was a very imaginative man," her mother corrected. "And I really don't know what your problem is. It's probably hormones, *late* hormones. Just remember that 'She who waits upon fortune is never sure of a dinner. The wheel goes 'round and 'round and some are up and some are down, and still the wheel goes 'round.' You're getting old enough to start having a little action for yourself instead of nagging me about mine. I only have a few years left for romance, and I'm not going to let a bellyaching physics major of a daughter cramp my style. I'm very careful about the men I bring home. I check them out very carefully to make sure that they're not going to run around here with an axe. I'm getting old and I need someone to hold me, and tell me everything's going to be all right. And you and I both know it's not going to be you, kiddo. So lay off, or move out. Do you hear me loud and clear? I love you, but I love myself just a little more. Got it?"

Sibella thought a moment. "Got it, Mom."

Mrs. Cametta grabbed the plastic bottle of Parkay and began injecting it into the English muffin. Sibella watched her mother's face twitch slightly as though there was still one more thing she wanted to say. Finally, her mother's mouth opened.

"You're a very pretty girl, Sibella," Mrs. Cametta said softly. "Someday *some* boy has got to like you."

Sibella got out of school at three-twenty, and by three-thirty she was at the Mariner's Harbor Midget Raceway on Lake Avenue. A high wire fence surrounded the huge piece of property. The main building was locked, but inside Sibella could see about fifty different kinds of pinball machines and electronic games. There was a long counter, and beyond that, picture windows looked out onto the raceway and small grandstand. A huge garage was attached to this building, protruding into the fenced area. *The repairs*, Sibella decided. *He must work there. He must come to this door mornings, walk past all those twinkling amusement games, turn right, and go through that door.* She could feel his spirit floating through the air. As scientific as she was, she did believe that presences could be felt. Her favorite short story was called "God's Talky Doll," in which a lady mental patient used to show up at a nightclub every day, and play on the piano to leave a message of love for an evening bartender. Maybe this boy, this incredible boy, would know she had made her first visit.

5

She checked Thursday in the morning before school, and again after school. There wasn't a light or a sound or a breath of life at Mariner's Harbor Midget Raceway. When they said only open on the weekends, they meant it.

Friday Sibella woke up late. She barely made it to school. In physics Mr. Brightenbach asked her to discuss the substances attracted by an electrified body. That's what she felt like herself, an electrified body. "And what is the magnetic variation where you live?" Mr. Brightenbach also asked. *Hope*, Sibella wanted to say, *hope is where I'm living now.*

School took so very long that day. In the cafeteria it took what seemed hours to get a piece of juicy meat that looked like filet of rodent. And she felt as though chemistry class was eight full hours making hydrogen sulfide. And all the teachers asked her to read or construct or recite or perform. Only in study could she check *How to Pick Up Boys* for the next chapter. Near the appendix there was an encouraging testimonial supposedly from a librarian's daughter. *"I'm not a great beauty. My nose is a little too big, and my bust is a little too tiny—but this has never stopped me from being one of the most attractive girls in my hometown. What I learned was that a girl has got to create her own good luck nowadays. Friends can be counted on to supply some boys, but the only way for a nice girl not to turn into a terribly lonely one is to take boys where—and that means anywhere—she finds them."*

At three-thirty she headed out the main entrance of the high school, lugging her toolbox, and turned in the opposite direction from home; and a full two blocks from the raceway she could hear the noise of the cars zipping, *roaring*. He would be there. The raceway was open and *he would be there*.

She had to walk along a full block of the fence before reaching the main building. Fifteen or so racers were zipping around the track, each paced a good distance from the others so the kids driving them wouldn't kill each other. Some of the drivers looked like they had rushed over from the third grade and bought tickets.

She went in the front entrance and decided she wasn't quite up to looking at the horde of boys playing the pinball machines. She focused in on the counter instead, where two young girls were snatching up the money from some other kids. The girls both had long straight blond hair, and they looked like twins. Somehow they managed the fine art of conducting business without taking their eyes off the boys at the pinball machines.

They both were yelling flirtatious remarks at one rather tall Irish-looking boy who spoke like he had already had a beer too many.

"Ya want laps?" one girl asked Sibella.

"Oh, it's the first time I'm here," Sibella explained. "I just wanted to..."

Already the girl had tuned her out and was moving on to the next kid.

Sibella decided she had better play a pinball machine before she was bounced for loitering. She moved to one that had Wonder Woman lit up and double flippers. She put a quarter in. The machine did some electronic chattering and shot a ball into the slot. She fired the ball and as it beat its way around under the glass she let her eyes look toward the door at the far end of the counter. She could see bodies moving in and out, a glimpse of a well-lighted garage beyond, and a few carcasses of partially assembled midget race cars. Images began to clarify. One boy with a baseball cap, it wasn't him. A girl doing a sort of twist while talking to another boy with glasses. This passage-way to the garage was obviously the *in* place to be. This was the equivalent to the booth right next to the jukebox at Steckman's. It seemed like proximity to machinery was always a criterion for status.

She began to feel very warm and opened her coat. Then she realized she was still holding her toolbox. She'd have to put it down, but she'd keep her left foot touching it so nobody could rip it off. A new figure had entered from the garage and was talking to the boy with glasses. At first he was in the shadows. The photo in the newspaper had not lied. The colors were slightly different. Everything about him was lighter. It was as though reality had made an adjustment, turned up a contrast switch. *He was the perfect boy.* His features seemed stronger now. A full smile and wide-open thirsty green eyes told her he was not a predator. He was the perfect weight, with a thick belt hugging his slim waist. The buckle announced in giant brass letters "DAN." He looked eighteen, tops. His sleeves were rolled up, and even the smudges of black grease on his arms and chin made him look like he had simply been anointed. She wanted to rush from the uncompleted pinball game into the passageway and hold him. She wanted to tell him that her bloodstream was gurgling like a brook. More than anything she wanted to hear his voice *clearer.*

She picked up her toolbox, moved nearer to the passage as though reading the advertisements circling the doorway. She was now less than five feet from him. His voice was solid, low. It was the right voice for his body. It was a voice to cherish. His feet—they looked like nice feet in nice shoes. He stood attractively. *A princely posture,* she thought. And the enthusiasm, a masculinity as though he was a young vendor selling grapes and luscious cherries on the street. Yet it all seemed so natural. His hands were on his hips. Now one was against the wall, a leg raised on a small stool. He was in motion, *alive.* His Western-style shirt was wrinkled.

The top two buttons opened showing a yellow T-shirt peeking out. He looked exactly like a Christmas present waiting to be unwrapped.

Suddenly a woman, about fifty years old, came out of an office just behind the counter. Sibella caught the name on the door: *Mrs. Fitzgerald—Manager.* She watched the woman strut in high heels, black dress, and sleek short hair. Her face was that of a sophisticated parrot with a nose and jaw that looked like it was about to peck.

"Danny," Mrs. Fitzgerald screeched over the din of the pinball machines. "Danny, I want to talk to you," she said, more like a command.

"Sure thing, Mrs. Fitzgerald," Danny said, snapping to attention.

"You did a swell job on the repairs, kid," the woman chirped. "I asked Louie, and he says you can move on to the new cars. He'd like to have them all assembled and on the track by Sunday latest."

Sibella watched Dan grab for a rumpled package of cigarettes. "I'm gonna need another swig of your Pepto-Bismol, if you don't mind, Mrs. Fitzgerald. I really tied one on last night," Dan said.

"Oh yeah, you just watch out, kid," Mrs. Fitzgerald advised. "If you make your last beer for the night one with an egg in it, it kills the gas."

"Thanks for the advice," Dan said appreciatively.

"Think nothing of it, sweetheart," Mrs. Fitzgerald said. She stuck a kiss on two of her fingers and slapped it against Dan's face, and then scooted back to her office.

34

One of the blond twins at the counter was now riveted on Sibella.

"Can I do something for you?" the girl wanted to know.

Sibella moved her toolbox from her left hand to her right. She tried to form words in her throat, but nothing happened.

"I said, do you *want* something?" the girl insisted on knowing.

Sibella knew she'd have to force herself. She pushed the air to the upper part of her lungs and then let it wheeze out. *"Dan,"* she said, so softly she knew it didn't have a chance to be heard over the din.

"Whatcha say?"

"I want to see *Dan.*"

The girl let out a knowing laugh and screamed to her countermate, "Hey, Janey, somebody to see Dan." They both let out a laugh. Sibella didn't have the faintest idea what was so funny.

The counter girl yelled down the passageway, "Hey, Dan, hey, Dan, one of your girl friends is here to see you."

Sibella wanted to die. What a cruel, horrible thing for that thin little blond witch to say. Dan had been heading back toward the garage. She knew he hadn't heard and decided to move straight down the passage toward him. She lost sight of Dan for a moment.

"Excuse me. Excuse me, please," she said, squeezing through with her fake fur and toolbox slapping into someone's knee. "Please excuse me."

35

Now she was in another doorway. The large garage ignited with the sun-strong fluorescent lights. It seemed empty. Nothing alive, only the carcasses of midget racecars.

"Dan," Sibella called too quietly. Then she said louder, more firmly, *"Dan!"*

She jumped as Dan came rolling out from under a blue race car. He had been working on a mechanic's dolly, and rolled toward her like a body on roller skates. He grabbed onto a fender and stopped. Still horizontal on the floor, he said. "You called me?"

"I wanted to talk to you."

Sibella's throat froze. She felt like she had just been dipped into a cryogenic bath, frozen alive. The only motion she could force was to hang her toolbox against her leg.

"Hey, look," Dan said, "I've got to get these two buggies finished. You're not supposed to be back here—insurance purposes, you know. What do you want?"

Sibella put the toolbox on a workbench. She opened it. "I have some tools. I brought some tools I've never used. My father works at a scientific company in New York and he gave me this set. They were a Lamborghini promo kit for pit workers in Monaco. The Grand Prix a few years ago. My father doesn't live with us, he's in New York," she found herself muttering.

She lifted out a plastic case of shiny precision tools: a timing key, a silver souvenir set of wrenches, a bevy of beautiful metallic assists to perfect borings and filings for plugs and valves, cams and cam shafts, pistons. "They're for you," Sibella said. "I'm not into race cars, but I thought you could use them. My father wouldn't mind." Still she was muttering.

Dan lifted himself from the mechanic's dolly and stood perpendicular. His eyes rolled over the tool set. He looked shocked.

"Look, I don't know what you've been smoking, but I'm in no mood for a freak trip."

Sibella felt her throat freeze again. She grabbed at it and shook it, making words spill out. She was more shocked than he was. "I'm sorry, I thought you'd like them. You'd don't have to accept them, but I just figured I'd never use them, and I thought you'd like them."

"I don't even *know* you," he said. "I don't know who you are. What's going on here? You're freaking me out, you really are. You're freaking me out."

Sibella put her gift back, picked up her tool kit, and clutched it tightly to her. She began to back toward the door. "I saw your picture in the paper," she wheezed, "and I thought you were someone I could talk to about gear ratios and . . ." She noticed his hands reaching up to his head, rubbing his temple as though a little massage would help him stop feeling that he was going mad.

"You saw my picture in the paper?" Dan asked, his mouth hanging open in disbelief. "You saw my picture and you figured I wanted *tools*?"

Sibella felt as though she would collapse. She turned and started into the passageway, but turned back around. "I'm planning to open a Mobil gas station and..." Now she was only able to exhale snippets of thoughts. "I go to Port Richmond High School. You have nice lights...."

Suddenly she was aware of the black, birdlike form of Mrs. Fitzgerald swooping behind her. Mrs. Fitzgerald yelled into the garage, "Hey, Danny, Lou wants to take his break now. Get out there, okay, hon?"

Sibella turned swiftly. She began to swim up the passage.

"Did you see that girl?" she heard Dan asking. "Did you see her?" "*Forget* the girls," Mrs. Fitzgerald ordered. "Just get out there."

In a moment Sibella was lost in the middle of ths pinball machines. She would hide behind the crowd and bombardment of sound, which was now of blurring intensity. She managed to slide into an instant-photo machine and pull the curtain just as Mrs. Fitzgerald and Dan came hurrying out. Mrs. Fitzgerald went into her office and shut the door. Dan kept going and went out the door to the track. Now he was wearing a McKee Vo-Tech jacket, which only made him appear even more princelike.

Sibella tucked her hair up under a wool skullcap. That would do it. He'd never recognize her. She could just go out and sit in the grandstand. The toolbox was the only giveaway, but she could put that behind her.

There were only about fifteen kids sitting in the grandstand. There was no wind, but it was still cold enough. She saw what had to be Louie talking to Dan for a moment. Then Louie ran inside and disappeared into Mrs. Fitzgerald's office.

Dan was now controlling the track. He had to put new customers into the race cars and collect their tickets every time they wanted to do a lap. She soon caught on to the procedure. There was a double pair of white lines, but only one race car at a time could fit. The front wheels had to be lined up on those white lines in order to signal a green light. When the green light flashed, that meant the proper interval had gone by before the last race car had left on the track. Leading up to the starting line were four lines at intervals. They were waiting positions. Then she noticed the helmet rack. Once the kids had their tickets, they ran to a helmet rack and picked out their headgear. Dan then told them which car to get into.

She thought Dan looked terrific against the bizarre snowscape, waving on the hot steaming engines with their drivers. A yellow scarf leaped around his neck as he twisted, jerked, turned left and right. His smile flashed. His eyes glittered. He was preening like a peacock.

A moment later she was aware of Louie bounding back out onto the track.

"Hey, you're screwing up the lineup," Louie complained.

"Look, I'm telling them what to do, but they're not smart, you know," Dan stated.

"You're not Einstein either," Louie explained. "That's why I spent three weeks showing you what to do."

"Look, I'll watch 'em, okay?" Dan said proudly.

"You'd better," Louie said and ran back inside.

"Step right up, folks. Step right up," Dan started yelling to no one special. "Everybody wins at the Grand Prix. Keep your eye on the computer read-out. Check your time. The record is fifty-one seconds. Try to beat the record." Then he did a little kick in the air.

Sibella adored his clowning. He put a couple of girls into race cars and collected their tickets. "Go directly to jail," he told them. "Do not pass go. Do not collect two hundred dollars." His laugh was so infectious, his wit so remarkable, Sibella decided. *He's compensating. He knows he's destined for bigger things*, she thought. This is only one pit stop on what will be a ride to his Racetrack of Destiny.

"Drive right past Princess Grace's palace, turn left at the pizza stand, and go straight to Rome for a little pinch," Dan yelled.

The girls in the cars were not amused, Sibella could see. But she thought it was marvelously funny, and now he was waving at the grandstand. She had always known she would fall in love with an extrovert. The green and scarlet colors of his school jacket were so theatrical. He was blowing kisses to the grandstand now. "I love you. I *adore* you. Thank you for generous attention and applause! May Kris Kringle be kind to you this year!"

A racer with a kid returned from a lap, almost running Dan over.

"Hey, dummy, you ought to stick to bumper cars."

"He's so forceful, Sibella realized—good-humored and forceful, a rare combination.

"Come on, twerps," Dan was yelling, flashing his big smile. He was so above it all. "Number-two spot, pull up to the number-two spot, dopey. 'Oh, I'm a Yankee Doodle Dandy,'" he started singing. "'Yankee Doodle do or die. Da, da, da, da,.'" A beautiful voice, Sibella realized. *Oh, my God, and he's dancing, and spinning*—a jump, a leap, a *split*!"

Louie was running down and yelling. "Don't freak out on me now, buster. I don't care how many beers you've had!" Dan began to speak very loudly, addressing the audience more than Louie. "I'm not freaking, Louie. Louie, would I freak out on you?"

"You're drunk again. I told Helen not to hire you."

"I'm not drunk," Dan protested. "Only my eardrums! They're the ones that drank all the beers. My eardrums need eight beers a night to put up with this noise. Besides, you said you wanted me lively."

"I said to show the crowd a good time," Louie brayed. "I didn't want you *idiotic.*"

Sibella noticed the joy flood suddenly out of Dan's face. Instantly, he looked sick, pained. He was hurtling to earth from such a joyous pinnacle. *He's so emotional,* Sibella worried, marveled. It seemed as though all the race cars had slowed to a halt. Dan seemed to be looking around for some sort of salvation. Suddenly he turned, and just pushed Louie aside. He marched toward the main building.

"Where are you going, jerk-o?"

"It ain't for Pepto-Bismol."

"You get back here in an hour or you're fired."

"You bet, Louie," Dan called back. "You just bet." And then he was zipping past the pinball crowd, past the twin blondes, and out the front door.

6

Sibella hit seven people accidentally with her toolbox as she raced after him. Outside, she saw him walking under a streetlamp near where Innis Street passed under the approach to the Bayonne Bridge. She rushed quickly after him, concerned that the clanking noise of wrenches in the toolbox would make him think a snowplow was bearing down on him. Before she could catch up to him, he turned into the Drop Inn.

Sibella halted outside of the saloon and peered through the red neon sign in the window. She could see Dan moving gracefully to the bar, ascending a stool. He looked so grown-up and smooth placing his order. Even in depression he was breathtakingly attractive. She felt as though she could do a complete term paper on the magnetism she felt toward him. He was a giant electromagnet and she was a helpless bag of iron filings. If he were to turn and look at her, she felt, her entire body would rise off the pavement and hurtle through the Drop Inn window. Rather than risk that, she opened the door and went into the bar.

She stood next to him, not approaching the bar, just *next to him*. There was a crowd of guzzling shipyard workers and some old guys from the Bethlehem dry docks. The bartender was so busy he didn't even notice her.

As if Fate had tapped him on the shoulder, Dan turned around. He must have felt her presence. He did a fix on her, and then looked back at his beer.

"Look, I've got some problems," he said softly. "Some stuff to work out. The last thing I need is a broad with tools."

Sibella admired how clearly he expressed himself.

Dan took a drink and looked back at her. "I don't need a monkey on my back, or whatever you've got in mind. *Comprende?* I'm in the twilight zone. Please do a scramo. One swift scramo coming up, okay?"

He was a little high, she knew. His eyes seemed to look past her out the front window, and latch onto the string of bridge lights. Then he snapped his head and chugalugged his beer. He snapped for a refill and downed half of that. Once more he looked at her.

"Do you have brain damage?" he inquired.

"You're *wonderful*," Sibella managed to utter just as the jukebox burst with a trio singing "laughing on the outside, crying on the inside..."

Dan started shaking his head, running his finger around the lip of his beer glass. He looked like he was in too much inner turmoil to protest any further.

Sibella stood her ground. She knew if ever she

needed courage, this would be the moment. This was the train about to leave without her. This was the boat sailing, and she would miss it if she didn't act. This was the turning point of her life. For the first time she'd have to utter clearly and quickly what was more important to her than any thought she had ever imagined.

"I love you very much," Sibella said.

Dan looked at her. A trickle of foam dripped down his chin.

Sibella knew it would be difficult for him to understand. She would have to be patient. She could see it from his point of view and knew it might take time.

"We're meant for each other, Dan," Sibella clarified. "At least I know I'm meant for you. I think you're a very fine boy, Dan."

"And I think you're missing a few marbles," he slurped.

"I want to help you, Dan. I want to devote my life to you. To help you reach the pinnacle of your chosen career. Dan, I know this sounds crazy, but when I saw your picture in the newspaper I . . ."

"Shut up," he requested. "Kindly shut up."

Sibella was thankful he wasn't looking at her now. But she knew he was listening. Now her words could come easier. "I watched you at the racetrack. You are destined for greatness. *You are a royal male who has been placed on earth to lead.* You are a gift to humanity. That Louie and Mrs. Fitzgerald don't appreciate you. I watched them. No one does. You're too good, Dan. I could help you achieve the mountains you wish to climb. Let me be the woman to drape myself on your gladiator's back and whisper, *'Thou wilt be king,'* whenever you falter. Whether your ambition is to win at Sebring, or to race at the Indy 500—or to burn rubber around the precipices of Monaco. Whatever your dream, I'll help it come true. I can change tires. I have some ideas for special fuels, carburetors, oil additives. I'll forsake my dream for yours."

Dan finished his beer. He stood up and walked right past Sibella. She stood still, watched his hand reach for the front door. Then he stopped, turned, and walked back to her. The red neon light streaming through the smoke from hours of burning cigarettes glowed behind his head, making him seem like a true divinity.

"What's your name?" he asked.

"Sibella. Sibella Cametta," she said, her lips twitching under his brilliant gaze.

"You're wacked out, Sibella Cametta," he offered. "You're really wacked out."

Then he was gone.

7

She got home before seven P.M. She was so excited, she didn't even mind her mother, or Charlie, or Maureen. Even dinner was terribly unimportant. The dream of Dan was all the nourishment she needed. Upstairs, later, she found her diary.

Dear Diary, today we met. He knows I'm alive. He's a dream come true, a darling, a prince with a grease gun. In his own sweet bashful way, he very much wanted to know my name.

She stopped writing. There was something different about her diary. It had been in the wrong spot in her bookcase. Somebody had touched her diary. Somebody had been *reading* her diary, and she knew very well who that was. She slammed the diary shut, charged out of her room, and practically kicked open the door to Maureen's bedroom. Maureen was alone, sipping a martini and putting on makeup.

"How dare you read my diary?" Sibella accused.

"I didn't read it, honey," Maureen said flatly. "I skimmed it."

"I can't have anything. You're back one day, and already you're snooping, messing around with my life. I don't grill you about Chucky. I don't snoop through your pocketbook or forage about in your Village apartment."

"Oh, Bessie, you're so sensitive."

"I am not sensitive. You're *in*sensitive."

"Chucky had to go up and check on the painters. They were doing a green trim in the hall. If there is anything that would make me barf, it's a green trim."

Sibella felt like going over, grabbing Maureen's cascading hair, and yanking it.

"Take a shower and get dressed. We're going out," Maureen ordered.

"Skippo," Sibella said. "Let's not and say we did."

"Look, Bessie, it's about time you learned a few things."

"From you? Ha, that's a laugh." Sibella made the mistake of hesitating. "Where do you want to take me?"

Within an hour Maureen had pulled out every sentimental gimmick in the book. First she had gotten Sibella to take a shower on the basis that cleanliness is *always* in order. Then she convinced her that she owed it to the world to do something about her hair. Then she owed it to to her mother to put on a little makeup, so that her mother would be proud to have a daughter; and then she convinced her that Sibella would be an absolutely cruel sister if she didn't come along with her to hear a little music in a delightful new club in St.

George called Chipmunks, "very au current and respectable," Maureen insisted. She would simply have to be more au current. By ten P.M. Maureen had them seated at a ringside table at Chipmunks.

"What is this, a ladies' club?" Sibella wanted to know.

Maureen had downed another martini, and gave a big spiel about new life-styles and being *open*, and the new role of the modern woman. Sibella decided that if the new role of the modern woman was to down four martinis in a half hour, she'd have to do without it. She found being dressed up interfering with her hearing, as though her entire mind was focused on the heinously yellow dress Maureen had poured her into. It had a diagonal neckline that gave her a distinct feeling she had just lost a Miss Arkansas contest, and she knew enough about cosmetics chemistry to know that her eyebrows were sporting a touch of graphite, her lipstick probably had a wax base derived from illegal sperm whale oil, and her mascara was really nothing more than colored shellac.

"You see, honey," Maureen was explaining, "when you finally do get a boy to go for the bait, you've got to learn to *do* things. You can't just lie back and rest like in the old days. I mean, if this boy is supposed to come back for second helpings, you're going to have to wiggle your tail a little. If he wanted a corpse, he'd go to a cemetery."

Sibella was thankful her sister was interrupted by the master of ceremonies on the microphone. He turned out to be the comedian. He did a lot of corny jokes, like "A bummer is not having a drop

of gin in the house and realizing why the kids'
lemonade stand was such a smashing success.
Ha, ha, ha!" All the ladies laughed. In a very
strange way, Sibella began to feel very uncomfortably
that almost everyone in the audience looked like
her mother. Those who didn't looked like her
sister. They all looked wired! Absolutely *wired*.

Finally the emcee finished. The drums began to
roll. The curtain opened. The women in the audience began to scream and shout. A parade of five
men came out and began to do bumps and grinds.

"This isn't what I think it is?" Sibella asked.

"Oh, it *is*." Maureen laughed. "Don't you just
love it?"

Sibella sat horrified. The men started to take off
articles of clothing. First a bow tie, then one took
off his jacket. One started to disrobe while doing a
tap dance. It seemed like the older the women in
the audience were, the louder they screamed.
One of the men started doing a disco, while
handing out bananas. Sibella felt as though she
was losing her mind. A woman sitting at a table
behind her knocked her with her elbow. "Look at
those legs!" she cried. "Holy garters! Look at
those *legs*!"

Most of the women stood and cheered and
yelled anything that came into their heads: "Honey, are you built! Whoopee!" they yelled at the
male exotic dancers. There were catcalls, laughter,
Bronx cheers. "You can leave your shoes under
my water bed anytime!" Maureen screamed to
one guy who looked like The Hulk.

Suddenly a face caught Sibella's eye. In the

lineup of male wigglers was one young boy. He looked about Dan's age. Darker hair, more delicate perhaps. He looked *totally* embarrassed, as though he were on the verge of tears at having to go out in front of that audience and strip to make money. He had his shirt off. The women were clapping. "More! More! Go, you hunk, go!" There was something cruelly tribal about the rhythmic stamping that seized the female audience. It was like a crowd had assembled for a stoning. Sibella couldn't bear to watch them zero in on the boy's discomfort and innocence. She stood up from the table. She was so furious she couldn't do anything but glare at Maureen. Then she shoved her way out through the sea of ladies. She'd gotten a full block away before Maureen was able to catch her.

"What'd you do that for? It was twelve bucks a ticket, you know," Maureen complained.

"I don't care if it was free," Sibella said.

"Look, Bessie, I'm sorry I read your diary. I did it for you. I said to myself, 'Oh my God, my poor sister is fifteen years old and she hasn't gone all the way yet.'"

"All the way!" Sibella practically screamed. "Did you see the face on that boy in there wiggling for all of you? Did you see that face? He was *dying*. I think there's a lot more important things in this world than going all the way, if you ask me."

Maureen let her cool down a while.

"Bessie," she finally started up, "you're missing out on so much. I just wanted to loosen you up, to see you happy. Honey, I don't care if you *do* end up running a Mobil gas station. I don't care even if you become the most famous astrophysicist in the world. You'll still need a little action or you won't be happy. Nowadays you can't let an erogenous zone go by."

"I'm not sure I even know what an erogenous zone is."

"I'll get you a book! You're got to check them all out," Maureen insisted. "You've got to attack with every inch of your skin. You've got to know how to make it a new and unique experience for a boy."

"Look, I'm a girl, not an *amoeba*." Then in a flash, Sibella was in tears. The tears rolled down as far as her chin before they froze. She didn't want to hear another word about Maureen's view on men. There was something missing. Something forgotten, as though Maureen had completely skipped over at least one man who was none of the things she said men were. Maureen was forgetting their father. Of course, her sister hadn't had that special connection with him that she did. Sibella was his girl. On the freezing street, with the Chipmunks sign blazing over her left shoulder, she remembered the sound of his step on the porch when he would come home from work each evening before the divorce. She would rush for her favorite spot for their nightly game of hide and seek. Always she'd hide under the daybed on the porch, the wicker daybed, and she'd watch his feet walk forward, then back, and she'd hear his wonderful voice saying, "Now where is little Sibella hiding? Where is she? *Where's my Sibella?*" Finally the suspense would kill her, and a burst of giggles would give her away. In a moment his smiling face would appear, horizontal on the floor. With his big wonderful eyes, he'd wink a few times and say, "Oh, there's my girl. *There's my little girl.*"

8

Sibella got up very early Saturday morning. She washed, put on her best slacks, a black turtleneck sweater, and a vest that had hundreds of tiny blue hearts on it. She looked in the mirror, and decided a little makeup wouldn't hurt. Shellacked eyes weren't all *that* ugly, and maybe Maureen had managed to bring the hair around to look like something other than blond linguine. She made it out of the house rather painlessly and then slid her way along the icy sidewalks, past the school, and on to the Mariner's Harbor Midget Raceway.

The track was open and the guy called Louie was testing out a car in the starting position. Inside, a handful of kids were already mesmerized by the pinball machines, and the lustful blond twins were very busy behind the counter preparing for the day.

"Is Dan in yet?" Sibella asked.

"Doesn't come on till four," one of the blondes said. She was wearing a button that said, *Free the Indy 500.*

"Do you have a phone number?" Sibella began

to stutter. "Maybe I could call him if you think he's up."

"Doesn't have a phone," Blondie Number Two said, ducking slightly and looking strangely out the picture window. *"And he's not up!"*

Sibella checked the direction where the girl was looking. Across from the racetrack was a dilapidated-looking building. All the structures on the block had been condemned or demolished, but this one stood out like a sore thumb. "Does he live there?" Sibella asked.

"If you want to call it that," the one with the button said.

"Thank you." Sibella pulled her fake fur closer around her. She was amazed how much warmer she was able to stay without having to lug the cold metal toolbox. She almost fell in the middle of the street, and again going up the few steps to the entrance of the building. The door was open. She went into the foyer. There were four apartments with buzzers. Apparently none of them worked, because the wires were all hanging out. Beneath one bell, written crudely with a pen, was the name *Dan Douglas*. What a brilliant name, Sibella thought, absolutely brilliant. Next to the name was scrawled *1A*.

Sibella pushed open the door into the inner hall. Apartment 1A was the apartment on the downstairs right. She rapped on the door, but there was nothing. She rapped again, but still nothing. She went back out and checked the writing on the bell. It was very clear—Dan Douglas lived in 1A, and unless there were two people with the name Dan in this tiny apartment house, she had to have the right apartment. She went back to 1A and knocked even more loudly. Then she began to call, "Hey in there. Hi! *Hello!*" She was really warming up now, and decided to knock more importantly. It was after *nine*. She was certain he would want to get up on such a beautiful day.

There was a creak. She knew life was stirring beyond the door. Slowly it opened. Dan stood there; the morning light rushed down the hall and flashed over his body. He was wearing jeans but no shoes or shirt. She had the strangest impulse to just reach out and touch his stomach, but she decided her hand was so cold he might buckle over with cardiac arrest.

"What do you want?" Dan wheezed, squinting at the bolt of light bouncing into his eyes.

"Did I wake you?" Sibella wanted to know.

"Oh, oh . . ."

"I wanted to apologize for the way I behaved last night," Sibella said. "I realize you must have really thought I was bananas."

"Oh, oh . . ." Dan muttered again.

"Can I come in?"

He looked too weak to answer, too cold and sleepy. He turned, leaving the door ajar. Sibella decided it was his own special way of inviting her to come in.

Stabs of light from the street bombarded through broken slices of shutter in the windows of the small studio apartment. Dan went back under the covers of the bed, which was nothing more than a mattress lying in the living room next to an old television set. There was a lot of exposed brick and a kitchen that looked as if it had been lifted out of a history book to demonstrate the conditions of living in the 1930's Depression. Clothes were draped on a partition, tossed into corners, and dangling off the arms of a stiff wooden chair. An open suitcase lay just outside the small bathroom. *Great men often have humble beginnings*, Sibella reminded herself. She watched Dan roll over and reach out to the little dented refrigerator. He grabbed a beer, propped himself up slightly on his pillow, and began to sip it.

"You want a beer?" he asked.

"No, thank you," she answered. "Do you usually drink this early?"

"Nope. I'm usually sleeping this early."

"How long have you lived here?"

"A couple of weeks. I had a friend, Johnny, who paid the rent for the month and he took off for Florida to drive nitroglycerin trucks. They pay two hundred bucks an hour if you live. At least that's what he told me."

Sibella decided this was the exact time she could use all the advice she had read on how to pick up boys. The way she had come on before was all wrong. *Subtleties*, a boy needs *subtleties*.

"Your hands look very strong," Sibella said. The book had told her this was an absolutely great opening line because it makes a boy feel powerful.

"Are you stoned?" he asked.

She decided she didn't hear his question. "You're a Pisces, aren't you?" The book had told her he'd be flattered by her interest and curious to know which one of his wonderful traits had tipped her off.

He took another swig of the beer. *"Why me?"* he asked, skipping right over Pisces. "Why did you have to zero in on me? Where do you live? Where do you come from?" He looked as if he was floundering in pain.

"I live over on Treadwell Avenue," Sibella said, delighted he was interested. "I live with my mother. My sister is staying with us for a couple of weeks." That was enough about herself. She'd better get the conversation back to him. "I'm sorry about last night, but I saw your picture in the paper. You looked like a nice person," she said, "and I just wanted to get to know you." The book had told her that no boy could resist the direct, honest approach.

"You carry around a toolbox for fun?"

"It's my career. I want to open my own gas station someday. I'm very good with my hands and..."

"I hated school," he cut her off.

"I saw your jacket. I knew a kid who went to McKee Vo-Tech. Snooky McAllister."

Dan exhaled a puff of smoke, grabbed onto the chair, and managed to stand. "Never heard of him." He stumbled into the bathroom and shut the door.

She heard water running, splashing. His voice came out through the door sounding like a seal barking. "I don't know what the hell *I* want to do."

58

"You're so young. Nobody's really supposed to know . . ."

"I'm *nineteen*," came Dan's reply, along with a few choking sounds.

He opened the door and came out drying his hair. If only Michelangelo or Van Gogh were there right now, Sibella knew this boy would be an inspiration for a mural called *A Prince Drying His Hair* or something.

"What are you staring at me for?" he wanted to know, checking his belly button and chest. "Do I have a cockroach on me?"

Sibella couldn't speak, such was the beauty of this boy before her.

"Hey, look. If I look beat, it's because I didn't get much shut-eye last night, you know, and I drank two six-packs of Michelob."

"You look fine," Sibella stuttered, "fine!"

Dan thought that over a minute.

"That's nice," he said. "Nice of you to say so." He took another swig of beer. "Hey," he said, "do you want to come look at a van with me?"

"I would like that very much," Sibella answered quickly.

"I told this guy I would look at his GMC 'seventy-one. It's got six cylinders, four speeds. He says it's got a sink, stove, ice box, the works, just smashed up a bit, and the transmission is sort of shot. He only wants a couple of hundred bucks for it, so I thought I'd check it out."

She felt like she was in a movie as she watched him finish getting dressed—that he had actually

59

asked her to *go look at a GMC van with him! It was their first date!* It was even better than that. It was as though all those dreams she had read about in teen movie magazines were coming true. All those dashing, smiling boy stars on the covers with the captions underneath would no longer be journalistic tricks. Oh no! Now when she looked at a super party issue of all those celestial celluloid boys, she'd know they really *could* be talking to her. "Sizzling hot pinups of all your faves—John, Greg, Rex, Scott, Leif, Andy, Mack, and more in this issue." That picture of gorgeous John and the quote beneath his sweet dimples: "Let's have a cozy picnic for two." Andy singing his heart out, a gold medallion around his neck: "Come with me on my love boat." Greg with a chimpanzee on the set, his lips open, hair bouncing with highlights: "Let's monkey around at the circus." And Matt, Matt who was the only one on television who even came near Dan in charisma; a photo of Matt saying, "Be my roller-skating date! Be my party girl." And the super teen contests: *Make your summer last forever—win a party on us. I'll sing my new love song just for you. Win my cuddly bear and the shirt off my back.* Those oh-so-adorable boys in the magazines that all the girls forked over $1.25 for. Oh, no, it wasn't exploitation! It was reality. If Dan Douglas could invite her to check out a GMC '71 value van, there was hope for every plain simple girl on earth.

The truck was in a junkyard on Richmond Terrace.

Sibella marveled at the way Dan spoke to the owner, a bear of a man who seemed really quite devoted to the scrap-iron business. He gave Dan the key. Dan motioned to Sibella for her to get in the truck with him. He started the engine, and in moments pulled the truck out onto Richmond Terrace for a test drive. The roar of its engine was deafening.

"I hope I didn't worry you too much about all those things I told you last night at the Drop Inn," Sibella yelled over the clanking.

"I don't even remember it," Dan yelled back. "I remember thinking you were Rebecca the Riveter or Sally the Spark Plug or something like that. Do you really know anything about motors?"

"Not much about race cars, but a van, that's more up my line. When my father was living with us, we'd always be in a shack out in the back taking something apart. We never got into high-performance equipment. Did they give you all that at McKee Vocational?"

"Your mom and pop are divorced?"

"Yes," Sibella said. "He works as a special researcher in New York, for places like Allied Chemical and companies like that—so I still go up to see him once in a while. You'd like him. He always helped me with school."

He shifted a gear and bellowed, "I hated school. I hated everything. Anything I ever learned was the hard way." Then he just changed the subject as though he couldn't bear thinking about school. "What do you think of this wreck? What do you think is wrong with it?"

"You really want to know?"

"Yeah."

"Well, the carburetion's way off—it's not letting the juice in," Sibella started. "And the ignition, it's not exactly lighting the fire, if you get what I mean. The compression is way off. If you're going to want this buggy to take you up any hills, you're going to have to add compression to put muscle in the stocker. Why did you hate school?"

"It wasn't just school. I hated everything and everything hated me.

"Where's your family?"

"They live out in Travis—just a couple of miles away. They're glad to be rid of me. My mother and father used to give me advice on everything. They were always talking about my future, always *my* future. They ended up ruining my present. They made me feel like I couldn't do anything, like I was a real waste. 'Oh, Doug, we know you're into drugs, Doug. Stand up tall, Doug. You look like a teenage hunchback. Don't drag your feet, Doug. Use your napkin, you're dribbling, Doug. You're disgusting the way you suck up your soup, Doug.' My father was worse than she was—used to keep records of my nail biting, and finger drumming, and feet tapping. 'Stop squinting,' he'd always say. 'Stop squinting and sniffling and twitching, and making those faces.'"

"But don't all parents do that?" Sibella sked.

"Not twenty-four hours a day. They got on my case so bad I used to lie down in bed and stare at the ceiling, and they would come in and ask if I had overdosed on something. Finally, my father just asked me to get out."

"Why?"

"Well, he said he was thinking about the whole thing, and he had decided that I was stupid and that there wasn't enough room for me in the house."

Dan stopped for a light, raced the engine for a moment. "Geeze, the valves sound rotten." The light changed and he shifted, and the van shot forward.

"He wanted me to work," he went on. "I can't hold a job. My mother wanted me out because she was into another whole trip of her own. They didn't know me. My mother and father didn't have the faintest idea who I was. They used to think I was just having a good time. I was Good-Time Danny, and life was a ball, that's what they thought. They didn't know how depressed I was about it. They didn't care that I was worried about getting old, and dying, and how ugly we all get along the way. Sometimes when I was lying in my bed, I would just shake because I knew someday I would have to die, and I knew that was going to be a bad trip. They thought I was really dumb, and I didn't think about the human condition. They didn't bother to ask me about my dreams where ugly Father Time would come after me with a hatchet and start slicing me into pieces. They never took me anywhere, so they didn't see me in a crowd or in an elevator with a pack of people. They didn't care about how horrible I felt that I was such a flop and a misfit. 'Always got pimples,' they'd say about me, or 'Use a mouthwash. You need braces. You got dandruff again! Your nose is too big. You're too thin.' Nobody bothered to build up *my* compression to get the fire going in the stoker. *No-sir-ee!"*

Sibella watched him grow silent. She was sorry now she hadn't interrupted him. He seemed to be falling now, falling into something very painful. She sat still for a moment, letting the noise of the engine and gears rumble through the van. She lifted her left hand and put it on his arm. She just wanted him to know that she was there and that she believed in him, and she would do anything she could to bring him the kingdom that she felt was rightfully his—*This lost and misbegotten prince,* she thought.

They were on Richmond Avenue now. He slowed, then stopped at a light. Steckman's soda shop was on the corner. There was a group of kids all in front watching the parade of dragsters. Now they were staring at the van.

"Mr. Steckman wants me to put in some fluorescent lights," she said. "Do you ever go into Steckman's?"

"Get out," Dan said.

Sibella thought she hadn't heard correctly.

"Please *get out.*" His request came more desperately.

Sibella waited a moment longer, opened the door, and stepped down into the slush of the street. Something told her she should just turn away then, that for some reason Dan needed sudden privacy and she shouldn't question it. It wasn't something she felt she should take personally. But perhaps he had been angry. She turned back, looked in the window. "Are you all right, Dan?" she asked.

The light changed, Dan accelerated, but not before Sibella saw the tears flowing down his face.

Her entry into her diary that evening came easily and simply: *Dear Diary, If I were to die now, I would want the world to know that I am more in love with Dan Douglas than I even dreamed....*

9

Sunday Sibella finished the fluorescent light installation at Steckman's. Then Mr. Brightenbach called and said he had driven up to Vermont for the weekend and that his wife was home and her car wouldn't start, so she went over and got that under control. Then Mrs. Russo had put her onto Mrs. Garibaldi, who wanted a bookcase just like the one she had done for Mrs. Russo, so Sibella took care of the measurements on that. In all she collected over thirty-seven dollars in payments and deposits, and she filed the money in envelopes. There was too much loose cash building up, so she'd have to make a deposit and start pulling down interest on it. But with every nail, every stroke of a brush, every moment of charging a battery—she thought about Dan. She worried about Dan.

It took her completely through the afternoon to finish the chores. When she got home, a sort of celebration was going on. It was a bit like a cocktail party in a singles bar. Maureen was giggling and undulating. Chucky was back, flexing his muscles. The disco music was blasting. Her mother seemed sweeter, even her boyfriend, Charlie, seemed kinder. *Like just plain folks*, Sibella thought. *Just plain folks trying to have a good time.*

She knew it was the sight of Dan's tears that had rendered her so compassionate, her sensitivity to everyone turned up to full power. Her sister, her mother and her boyfriend—they were being lovely to each other, and they were being lovely to her.

"Have I got a surprise for you," Maureen said, giving Sibella a big hug and kiss.

"I don't think I can take any more surprises," Sibella said.

"Oh, Bessie, you just get scrubbed up, paint up that face, and put on a smile. Good things are going to happen to you tonight," Maureen said.

"We're not going to Chipmunks again?"

"I love your sense of humor, Bessie. Love it," Maureen repeated. Sibella went upstairs, got showered, dressed, put on a little shellac and beeswax. She only had one real dress left, and it was so frilly, she felt like the farmer's daughter in it. Finally she sat on the edge of her bed and decided maybe she should just write some more in her diary. If she waited long enough, maybe they would forget about her downstairs. Then she could mosey on over to the midget racetrack around ten. But the music was blasting even louder and the laughter from downstairs reached deafening decibels. Finally the doorbell rang and she heard a climactic scream from Maureen resound up through the floor. Moments later there was a frantic set of footfalls heading up the stairs. Maureen flung open the door. "Come on, honey, *this is it!*"

"What do you mean, 'it'?" Sibella wanted to know. Maureen grabbed her hand and yanked her up off the bed, out the door, and down the stairs.

"Sibella, I want you to meet Bertram."

Sibella blinked her eyes. *Oh-oh*, she thought. *Now it's a blind date.* She looked at the puzzled boy before her and decided she'd better say something.

"Hello, Bertram," Sibella said, aware that Maureen, Chucky, her mother, and Charlie were all lined up as though waiting for some tremendous reaction out of her.

"Bertram is Chucky's brother, seventeen. Isn't he a doll?" Maureen insisted on knowing.

Sibella looked at the doll. Actually, he *was* a doll. He had all the strength and good looks of Chucky, but it looked like he had a brain as well. His eyes were sweet, yet clear and focused. His hair was not all that much unlike Dan's, but groomed, locks falling with handsome casualness. He spoke some sort of greeting to her, but she was so surprised at the kindness and warmth of his smile that she didn't hear.

"Make yourself comfortable in the TV room, and we'll bring you some drinks and *hors d'oeuvres,*" Maureen insisted, whisking the two of them onto the wicker daybed. "Be right back," she said, zipping out and closing the French doors behind her.

"Excuse me a moment," Sibella said, scooting right after her. She caught Maureen by the stairs. "Do you mind telling me what's going on?"

"That's Bertram. He's for *you*, honey, *for you*," Maureen explained.

"He doesn't even *know* me."

"He'll love you, honey, I know it."

"He's going to be bored stiff with me."

"Bessie, trust me, just trust me." She took Sibella by the arm, led her rapidly back to the daybed like a matron controlling a prisoner. When the French doors were closed again, it was just Sibella and Bertram, *alone*. "I'm really very glad to meet you," Bertram said. His voice sounded sincere.

"I didn't know Chucky had a brother," Sibella said nervously. Her eyes now moved down his neck to his shirt, a perfect shirt, a gorgeous collar, and a crew-neck sweater that looked like he'd gone to Brooks Brothers and checked every weaving to make sure not a single thread was out of place. He seemed too good to be true, as though he was born to be perfect, born to be paid great sums of money to do nothing but stroll through expensive stores and buy fine things.

"Chucky told me Maureen had a nice sister. I think he was right," he said directly.

"You seem very nice to me, too," Sibella said. Then she let the small talk go on for a while. *Oh, my God, he's such a beauty. He's so sympatico.* She began to sense that she was in the presence of another prince. She started to feel guilty about it, as though in some way she was being disloyal to Dan. Dan needed her, this boy didn't. She couldn't help wondering how much easier it might have been if she had met Bertram first. She became excited as she began to plan what she would write

69

in her diary that night. She'd say, Oh, Diary, my sister is the most wonderful girl in the world. I think her mean vicious sibling-rivalry period is over, and she's at last able to open up and share with me. Tonight she brought me a most kind and loving boy. I am the ugly duckling next to him. He is all that Dan is without the depression. Bertram is smart, going to be a lawyer. I could run a chain of gas stations. I could invent new fuels and he could do the patents on them, and sell the subsidiary rights. . . .

Maureen tiptoed in with two glasses of white wine and some shrimp *hors d'oeuvres*, and then scooted out with a wicked little smile on her face.

Bertram had moved closer, put his arm behind her against the back of the daybed. She felt protected, too *intimate* to eat shrimp. He was moving so fast, so incredibly fast, she thought. *I'm being swept off my feet*, she told herself. *The chemistry must be breathtaking. Oh, my stars, thank you. This is how I dreamed life would be. I'm not forgetting Dan, I swear I'm not. My feelings are with Dan, but Bertram is Speedy Gonzales. I know Dan and I have a destiny together, but maybe there's some way I can keep this one warming up in the bullpen just in case.* She hated herself for that thought. She would have to be more honest and risk disappointing Bertram.

"Your eyes are cute," Bertram said, his lips moving closer to her face.

"You're very nice to say things like that," Sibella said, her breathing deepening, "but I've got to tell you I'm already in love with someone. I don't feel right letting you go on like this. I know that any
70

girl in the world would think I'm crazy, but I would be playing with a stacked deck, and I'd feel, I hate to say *immoral.* But I've had fifteen years without action and suddenly I'm getting more than I can handle."

"I don't understand," Bertram said.

"What do you mean, you don't understand?"

"Your sister told me you didn't have any boyfriends."

"Well, I *had* nobody," Sibella said, and then she realized there was something a little strange. "Why did she tell you I had nobody? What did she do, say I was desperate? That's what she said, didn't she? She said, 'Hey, Chucky, I have a little charity work for your brother.' *Is that what she said?* And I don't mean that to be cruel. I don't want to sound like I'm angry or anything, but isn't that what is going on? That *is* what's going on, isn't it?"

Bertram looked a little sheepish—not very sheepish, just a touch. Even this embarrassment he would be able to handle with aplomb, Sibella suspected.

"I know you're a nice guy," Sibella said. "And I'm not angry or hurt. Just level with me, will you?"

"You won't tell them?" he asked.

"I won't tell them."

"I believe you," Bertram said. Then he *did* sound embarrassed. "They gave me a hundred dollars."

"One hundred dollars!"

"You are angry, aren't you?"

"One hundred United States dollars?" Sibella repeated. "I can't believe it."

71

"Yeah, but if you tell them I'll have to give it back. I'm supposed to just give you a few kisses and feels for an hour. I was supposed to light up your life. Please don't tell them I told you." She could see he was genuinely sorry.

"I won't," she finally was able to say.

"You *are* hurt, aren't you?"

Sibella hesitated, really thought it over. I'm *not* hurt. Actually I think for the first time in my life I'm feeling a sense of love for my sister. I had no idea she'd ever pay a hundred dollars to make me happy. Break my legs, yes; make me happy, no." Now the only thought in her head was how quickly she could make it to the Mariner's Harbor Midget Raceway.

"See you, Bertram," she said, grabbing her coat and heading straight out the door. "And don't worry about it. My fur's a fake, too—and I still like it!"

10

By eight-thirty she was playing the Wonder Woman pinball machine, mixed in with the horde of other kids. The blond twin sensuous teenage counter girls were selling tickets like crazy, and the passageway to the garage was buzzing with flirts. Sibella saw Mrs. Fitzgerald zip out of her office a couple of times, and once caught a glimpse of her shooting some orders at Dan. Sibella would wait. He'd have a break soon, she was certain.

Sibella played a game in which depth charges were released from a submarine, and they blew up battleships on a screen. Then she played an electronic intergalactic-war machine, and after that she sat in another machine where she drove a little fire engine up and down electronic streets, trying to avoid collisions. Finally, Louie came growling in and told Mrs. Fitzgerald he wanted a break. She ordered Dan out onto the track. Sibella put her coat and gloves on. She took her place in the viewing stands. It looked to her as though half of Port Richmond High School had come out for a

Sunday night race around the track. *Anything to avoid homework,* she thought.

Dan looked very depressed to Sibella. He didn't smile. He behaved like a robot. He made the kids pick the right-size helmet. He stuck them in the cars, put on their safety belts. Even when one kid's car chewed up a half dozen rubber cones in the homestretch, he hardly reacted. For the first time in her life she wished she had a toolbox with wrenches to fix human machines. She was in love with a very troubled boy, she knew. That she could even have considered anyone else for a fleeting moment was absurd. This boy in the McKee Vo-Tech jacket, waving, calling out starting spots, pocketing tickets—this boy puffing hotly in the cold wind—*was her boy.* He had cried for her. He trusted her enough to cry. Soon she would be in his arms. They would hold each other, comfort each other. Now it was only time keeping them apart.

Louie came back in about twenty minutes this time. Sibella knew Dan hadn't seen her yet and watched as he shot back into the main building. She scooted after him.

"I'm getting a beer," Dan yelled to Mrs. Fitzgerald.

"Okay, honey," she shouted back to him over the din.

Sibella caught up to him before the first streetlight. "Dan!"

"Oh, it's you."

Sibella ran to keep up with him. "Did you buy the van?"

74

"Nope. I don't have any money. I don't buy vans, I just look at them."

"I'm sorry if I asked too much about your family," Sibella said softly. "I'm really sorry."

"Forget it," Dan said, pushing open the door to the Drop Inn. Sibella just managed to catch the door before it slammed on her. Dan slid into a booth on the side. She slid in across from him, staying in the shadows so the barmaid wouldn't see she was underage.

"Do you want a beer?" he asked.

"Yes, thank you," Sibella said, though she really hated beer.

"Two beers," Dan ordered. In a moment there were two big mugs foaming on the table, and two very silent kids.

"Are you stoned?" Sibella finally asked, noticing Dan seemed fixated on a backlighted poster showing horses pulling a cart of beer kegs.

Dan just looked at her. Then suddenly he opened up a wonderful smile. Sibella now felt the same magnetic pull as when she had first seen him on the sports page. Only she was seeing him in graeter detail. She was more relaxed, in the light of this smile, able to define her attraction more clearly. His jacket was open, arms spread along the back of the booth. He was wearing a flannel shirt, little yellow plaid stripes running through a dark fabric. His neck was beautiful to her. The buttons seemed to hug the shirt to his chest, except one button which was open and she could see the skin of his stomach. He still smiled at her, silently smiling. What she saw in his face was what she thought was the definitive clue to the difference between a boy and girl. She felt as though she was discovering something no one else had ever observed. That she was Darwin, and Dan was her Galápagos Islands. What Dan had on his face was a type of *freedom*. Not that he didn't have his own baggage of problems, but more than any single thing, that's what a boy really was. A boy was *freedom*. Dan's mouth was open just far enough to show his shiny white teeth. His eyebrows were very dark and full, and his eyes said something like, *Well, girl you've seen my depression, you've seen my problems, but I'm a boy and I'm throwing them off. There's life in me, girl. There's more life than you'll ever know with your curse of eyebrow pencils and lash shellac and fragrance fears. My pain lifts from me. I am a deer, a buck with many horns, the great male teen machine. You will forget you've ever seen me cry. I am good-time Danny. If the shelf life of a Twinkie is twenty-five years, I could last fifty. I could lean forward over these fears and digest you with kisses. My clothes, my mouth, my eyes, are pure promise. I am a boy, still lord of the earth.*

"Why are you smiling?" Sibella finally asked.

"Because you look so serious. You look as though you *are* in love with me."

Sibella lifted the mug to her lips, took a good slurp, and wiped the foam off her nose.

As the fluid ran down her throat, she vowed to resist further every ladylike convention that had been heaped on her back. "Every molecule of my body and mind is being pulled toward you, Dan,"

she said. "You make me feel electric. I want to
kiss your neck, touch your brow. I feel like a
planet in the gravitational pull of a star. You make
tigers dance in my brain. I would stand on one
finger, if you asked. I would be fired from a
cannon. I would do anything you asked me in the
center ring with all the world watching. I'm so
proud to be here. I would give up every dollar I
had in the bank. I would quit school. I don't care
about a Mobil gas station or a career. I feel tears of
joy dancing behind my eyes. I'm not at the Drop
Inn. I'm next to you and a great circus horse is
waiting. The horse is waiting and I'm so terrified
about what your next words will be. The dream,
the sparklers, the tubas. I've conveyed to you the
speed at which I'm traveling. I am beyond the
speed of sound. I am coming to you at the speed
of light. You are Einstein, you are radium, you are
all my mind can conceive," she managed to say
into his smiling face.

Dan looked incandescent, still. She knew her
words had fed him and now she waited. She
sipped her beer, then just looked into his eyes.
Finally he broke the stare, took a sip of his beer.

"You make me feel naked," he said.

"I don't mean to."

His smile went away. He took another mouthful
of beer and savored it, and swallowed.

"Why are you in such a hurry?" he wanted to
know.

"I don't think it's a hurry."

"You talk about me like we're going on Star
Trek or something."

"Dan, please tell me how you feel." She felt begging creeping into her voice. "I could help you, I really could. We could help each other."

Dan looked at his beer. He wiggled a cigarette out from his sleeve and lit it. "Look, Cametta, it's nice of you to even notice me. There is something nice about you, or I wouldn't let you con me into listening to that spiel."

"Did I con you?"

"Look, I'm flattered, I really am, but I don't think you're seeing me very clearly. I'm not exactly the celestial orb you're getting all steamed up over." He took another deep drag on the cigarette. "You see, you're sort of forgetting one thing—I'm a bum."

"You're not a bum."

"Take my word for it, I'm a bum. Everybody else knows I'm a bum. You've got some sort of cataracts or something. I'm not flying to any moon. My life isn't going anywhere. I can't do diddly-do, and it's taken me a good long stretch to deal with it."

"You're not a bum."

"I mean, I wanted to be someone. I remember that, but who doesn't? Half the kids at McKee Vo-Tech wanted to be someone, but I'll tell you where I'm going to end up—with a big zero." Dan suddenly looked very depressed. "Life is stupid, Cametta. And if you've got yourself tricked into any kind of trip over a gas station, if you're *psyched up* over anything, you ought to keep that little trick going." He leaned back and flashed a slight smile. "I'm not one of the great bellyachers.

A lot of people got a lot more chances than me. But school sucks. Every public school sucks. I sat around for ten years and never had a one-to-one with a teacher or anybody who cared. All they did was keep passing me. They made believe I wasn't there. Nobody even went home to my house to say, 'Hey, your kid is a big waste and we've got to fix it now.' Nobody ever asked me if I was ever interested in anything. I don't even remember if I *was* interested in stuff. The way I see the world now, everybody is worried about themselves. Nobody really wants kids anymore. They're all worried about good salaries and their pensions, like everybody is living in coffins. So busy living in coffins, all they have is a big belly laugh whenever anybody talks about the future. Oh, the kids of the future generation, *hah!* I can just see my mother and father sitting around the television saying, 'Whoopee, we got to look out for the kids because they're our future generations!' There is no future generation. *There never will be anymore because nobody cares about one.*"

Sibella breathed deeply. She still felt like a planet falling toward this star, but the star was diminishing. Somehow she would help it burn again. She knew she wouldn't stop until she could bring it back to its rightful brilliance.

"You must believe in something," she said. "God or love, or engines or something."

"Oh, I do," he said. "I believe in a Surfer van. I believe in red carpets and custom paneling. With a gaucho bed and bay windows, and it's got to have AM-FM stereo, eight track. That's what I believe in. And it's got to have an overhead console, blue, I know it's a blue job, mag wheels, and radial tires. It's also a V-eight. I know exactly what I believe in because I saw it at Del Amor Dodge on Victory Boulevard. That's what I believe in—a used Dodge Surfer van."

"If it means so much to you, couldn't you save money from your salary? Put down a deposit. They could hold it," she said. "You could get a loan."

"Look, I'm not asking for pity, or advice on how to buy a van. I can barely pay the next month's rent and buy a couple of beers. I just told you that because that's my ambition. I thought you'd better understand that before you go any further into orbit over me. *Boom!* I've been blown up. You're sitting with the original big-bang theory. It's over for me, Cametta. I was killed off in the third or fourth grade. *They* made me a loser. It's all passed me by. I missed the boat. You're looking at an old crankshaft. I'm not crying in my beer to get sympathy from you. I just want you to know I don't understand your wavelength. You've got me mixed up with somebody else. I don't believe in love. I believe in a Dodge van. My entire plan for happiness is to have this van, and go beat on it in the woods. I want to ride it out onto the mud flats when the tide goes out. I want to fish from it. I want to live in it. More than anything, I want to die in it."

They sat there for several minutes sipping their beers. Sibella didn't know what to say. Obviously she had said too much, but he didn't get up and run away, and he didn't tell her to leave him alone.

"Come on, I'll show you a good time," he said suddenly, his smile back. He threw the waitress a couple of dollars, and Sibella had to run to keep up with him. He began to jog in the opposite direction from the racetrack.

"Where are you going?" Sibella asked, jogging alongside him.

"You'll see."

She actually enjoyed jogging with him. A little portion of her mind worked out a fantasy whereby they were already married and living in a very large castle on Grymes Hill. They were a royal couple who jogged around the castle grounds, and on this night they had simply decided to hit the lowlands to see what the common people were doing. They jogged by lots selling Christmas trees. She had totally forgotten about Christmas. It seemed it was easier to forget about every year. Jogging with Dan made the rows of Christmas trees look enchanted. Strings of lightbulbs fluttered over the treetops. Men stood around large metal cans with fires burning in them, rubbing their hands to keep warm like witches, warlocks. They jogged all the way to Bay Street, but from a mile away she suspected their destination. This late on Sunday night there was only one place open that far from Richmond Avenue—Wing Brothers Used Cars. She always saw their ads on television, with a couple of nice men walking around the lot pointing to bargains of the day: "Come down and see us. We're open 24 hours a day. Come on down and pet Al's pussycat." Then they would show what their pussycat looked like. It was a huge mountain lion that looked bored but healthy. Their commercials were so awful that everybody knew Wing Brothers had to write them themselves. They would always end up by showing their probably illegal pussycat in some new bizarre location, like under the hood of a station wagon, or with its head out of a vent of a motor home.

The entry in her diary would read, *We dashed over the snow like reindeer on their way to the top of the mountains. They were so happy to see us at the used-car dealer, especially when Dan told them he wanted to test drive one of their most expensive vans. He was so imaginative and creative telling them his father wanted to buy it for him for Christmas and that they had been away in Australia for over a month and this was the first chance he had to come down. I saw their mountain lion in a cage in the office, and petted it. It seemed very sad and wanted to get out. But one of the Wing Brothers told me it had to stay near the heater, or it would get pneumonia....*

What her diary would not record, because she did not want to leave a legal record of it, was what happened when the dealer put Dan in the driver's seat. The dealer sat next to him, Sibella sat on the seat right behind him. Dan had started the car and begun to move the van toward the exit of the lot when he braked suddenly and began to choke. He coughed and sputtered and choked so hard Sibella and the dealer became alarmed.

"It's nothing," Dan said. "My doctor makes me take these pills." He pulled a yellow-looking tablet from his pocket and threw it into his mouth. *"I can't swallow it. I need water, water!"* he cried out.

"Just a minute!" The dealer jumped out of the van and dashed into the office and began to fill up a paper cup at the water cooler.

"Hold on," Dan yelled at Sibella. He floored the accelerator so hard that the van leaped forward, slamming the door on the passenger side.

"What are you doing?" Sibella yelled, turning to see Wing Brothers quickly disappearing in the rear window. She was shocked, but probably not as shocked as she saw the dealer was, rushing out of the office, holding the little cup of water, and yelling, "Come back! Come back!"

Sibella leaned over the front seat to see Dan's face. *"Are you crazy?"* she asked.

He started to laugh and stuck his tongue out at her with the yellow "pill" hanging on the end of it. It was an M&M! He bit into it and started chewing it. Sibella slid into the front passenger seat.

"You're stealing the van! *You're stealing it!*"

"I am not!" he said, still laughing like a hyena. "He said I could take it for a test drive, so I'm taking it for a test drive."

"He'll call the police."

"Look, you heard him say I could take it for a test drive. Don't worry about it," Dan said, motioning her to calm down. "I do this twice a week."

"What about the racetrack? Don't you have to go back to the racetrack?"

"Nope. I was fired. Lou made sure they gave me notice. It was him or me—so it was me."

"Fired?"

"Yeah, tonight was my last night."

Sibella held on tight as he slid around a corner and began to barrel down Richmond Avenue. Several Christmas shoppers were still stumbling out of stores, their arms loaded with packages and dragging shopping bags. Kids were throwing snowballs outside of Steckman's, and a string of hundreds of Santa Claus forms hung from telephone poles straight down to Richmond Terrace. Sibella breathed deeply again and cracked her window slightly. She turned to see if they were being followed, expecting to hear police sirens at any moment.

"They dumped me because they said I didn't know what I was doing. That I was unemployable. I agreed with them," Dan elucidated.

"What are you going to *do*?"

"I was thinking about selling Eskimo Pies in Miami, going mineral hunting in Arkansas, or maybe working on a whale-watching boat. I think ice cream in Miami's my best bet, though."

"Dan, you've got to bring the van back."

"Relax, Cametta, I've got it all under control. I always ditch 'em and then call in and tell them where to find the van."

"Where are we going?"

"Del Amor. It's definitely a Del Amor night."

He raced the car along the Terrace, cut up Jewett Avenue, and turned onto Victory Boulevard. He stopped in front of Del Amor Dodge. It was closed, lifeless except for the signs in the windows screaming "Liquidation Sale" and "10%

Financing Available." There it was, Dan's dream—the used Surfer van with the carpets and custom paneling and the rear gaucho bed. The bay windows were done in stained glass.

"Yep," he said. "AM-FM stereo, eight track, V-eight. Look at the overhead console, the works."

Sibella looked at the van sitting in the shadows of the lot behind high fencing.

"Isn't she a beauty?" Dan sighed. "A *dream*. Me out here in a swiped van and that beauty in there. You see, that's what life really is, Cametta."

"I'm not sure I should draw you out on that or not," Sibella said, becoming a little concerned about the almost religious tone of Dan's voice as he beheld the Surfer van.

"See, that's where you are financially naïve," Dan explained. "You got all your little trinkets to believe in. You carry around a knockout of a toolbox. You've probably got a mother and father who made sure you always had Easy Street since they first popped you out. Your old man's probably pulling down a wad of loot and your mother's probably working, too."

"Not quite," Sibella said.

"But close enough," Dan insisted. "You see, when you grow up with nobody caring about you, no money, you're stuck. They ought to have a course in kindergarten—Beginning Money they should call it. *And they should have told me what was going to happen*, so I could have grown up without..."

Sibella watched his gaze lock onto the blue van. His eyes glistened.

He threw the shift into first and spun over the gutter ice, back out into the middle of Victory Boulevard. She saw him check his watch.

"Look, Cametta, I've got to ditch *this* van before the cops tag it. I'll drop you off."

"No. I'll stay with you till you get rid of it."

He gave her a wink and flew along the streets back to Mariner's Harbor.

The Drop Inn was still open, but the racetrack was closed as they rolled along Lake Avenue. He pulled the van to a stop. They closed the windows and locked the doors. He left the keys above the driver's sun visor.

"I'll call 'em from the bar. They always have an extra key. They just come pick it up, and chalk it up to one more teenage nut."

"I'll buy *you* a beer this time," Sibella suggested.

"Well, it's getting late—maybe some other time. You better go home before your folks get worried."

"I'd really like to talk to you some more. I'd like you to know a little bit more about *me*."

She couldn't help herself, she reached out and took his hand. She believed what she was going to tell him, and she wanted him to believe it, too. "You've got a terrific life ahead of you. You'll have everything you want. You've got so much to believe in. Let's talk about it."

Dan hesitated a moment, checked his watch. "Some other time, Cametta," he said, turning and disappearing into the Drop Inn.

Sibella stood, shivering in the cold. She pulled her phony fur close around her. She felt she couldn't leave. He had looked ready to break down again. Now was when he would need her most. She made her left foot move forward, then her right. Now she was walking. She reached to open the tavern door when she saw through the window: Dan was at the bar, his arms around a woman, an older woman. Sibella stopped, leaned closer to the glass at the door. The red neon flashed against the ice crystals on the window, but she could see clearly enough the short hair, the birdlike profile—*Mrs. Fitzgerald had her arms around Dan.* She was kissing him and he was kissing her. No wonder Dan had kept checking his watch. Her prince had had a date.

11

The beginning of the school week was absolutely
unbearable for Sibella. Mr. Herbert had agreed to
let her demonstrate a lycopodium explosion by
blowing through a rubber tube into a five-gallon
tin can. This was to release a cloud of pollen dust,
and a burning candle inside the can would trigger
an explosion blowing the lid off the can. Unfortu-
nately Sibella had put the top on too hard, and
held the tube too long, so a blast of lycopodium
came shooting back down the tube and into her
lungs. She had hardly finished recovering from
that when Mr. Brightenbach asked her to wire an
electromagnet in a way so it could demonstrate the
difference between a gong wiring and a bell wiring.
She was so out of it she could only produce a
gong and couldn't make a bell ring for the life of
her. Retarded, she felt completely retarded and
out of sorts. Then complaints came in from Mrs.
Russo that the staining was uneven on the
bookcase she had installed. The fluorescent lights
at Steckman's needed a new charger. Mrs. Blizinski
wasted an hour on Tuesday by cornering Sibella

and telling her all about the problems she was having with mildew fungus on her begonias. It was one catastrophe after another. But the major horror was lurking ahead. She would have to plead guilty to appearing moody. Her mother and sister and Charlie had every right to keep asking what was wrong with her. She had been short of temper. She had been sarcastic. She had refused to eat. By Thursday she came home from school and just stayed completely in her room.

"What's the matter?" everyone wanted to know.

"Nothing," Sibella had said.

Later she thought perhaps she would watch a little television. She opened the door to her room, walked out onto the landing. She could hear voices drifting up from the living room. At first it sounded like a soap opera on television. She could catch only a phrase or two as she started down the stairs, but by the time she reached the bottom, she was paralyzed with outrage. She realized the voice was Maureen's. Maureen was performing some very familiar words, and making comments like:

"She's just in love. That's all there is. Don't you remember when you were in love, Mom? Just listen to this: *'Dear Diary, I worship him. I pray for him. I ask God to be kind and watch over him. In my dreams I count the stripes in his plaid shirt. His belt buckle is branded on my heart. I dream only of placing my head on his chest, of kissing his . . .'*"

Mrs. Cametta was the first one to see Sibella. Charlie was the next. He at least cleared his throat, trying to signal Maureen to put down the diary.

Chucky elbowed Maureen and she looked up to see her sister.

Sibella tried to make sounds come out of her throat. At first it was only a gasping for air, but the gasps turned into great convulsing sobs. She came forward. Maureen was saying something about that it was all for Sibella's benefit, that they were all so *worried* about her. Sibella simply took the diary, turned around, and cried pathetically all the way up the stairs to her room. She held the diary to her heart as she fell onto the mattress. Maureen was right behind her.

"Darling," Maureen said, almost nonchalantly, "we were *just* trying to help. Everyone is terribly moved by your condition. We all know what being in love for the first time is like. It is so *hard*."

Sibella moved her hands to her ears. She had to turn her face from the pillow in order to get oxygen to stop her heart from cracking.

"It's so physical," Maureen went on. "You're just in love with him *physically*. He's a jerky little grease monkey, but that's what happens when you fall in love. The person you're in love with isn't even real. That boy isn't real at all."

"You killed me," Sibella said. "You're a cruel, spiteful killer. You're not my sister. I've never had a sister."

"Oh, Bessie, now at least that we really know what the problem is, we can fix it."

"How? Are you going to give Bertram another C note?"

"Look, Bessie, there's a lot more fish in the sea.

90

If you give me a little time I can find a hundred boys who would like to make it with you."

"I don't want someone to make it with me. I want someone to *like* me!"

"Look, you're fifteen. You're not even on the pill."

Sibella sat up in bed. She screamed, "I've got feelings, Maureen! I am a human being with feelings! And you are an overpainted, underdressed, cascading-haired *ass*!"

"Now, you wait a minute, little Miss Muffet," Maureen said, turning her guilt into rage. "How the hell much longer do you think you're going to run around being little Miss Tool Chest? What are you going to do, marry a *hinge*? Date a *screw*? Look, Bessie Big Bolts, you've got no friends! You haven't got a girl friend, a boyfriend, not even a dog friend! You spend your life clodding around with those physics and chemistry books and the nails and nuts, letting a hammer express your libido. Well, I've never had that problem. You're just green over it, aren't you?"

Maureen tossed her hair and stormed closer to the bed. She was absolutely furious. "I'll tell you what you can do with your wire cutters! You *like* being a professional virgin with everyone always having to feel sorry for you because no one can bear to take you out or get close to you. The only way to get a boy to stick on you would be with Krazy Glue. We're all tired of having to worry about your dateless diary, crammed with all those freaky *unrealistic* expectations."

Maureen suddenly stopped shouting. She just stood there. Sibella fell back onto the pillow, refusing to look at her. They did nothing for five minutes except breathe. Not a word. Not a tear. Nothing.

"Look, kid," Maureen said, now quite sadly. "I'm sorry the first boy you fell in love with turned out to be a dumb nurd."

12

Friday morning during breakfast Sibella told her mother she wasn't going to school. She was going to go to New York. She knew her mother would understand what that meant.

"Yes, it's been a long time," Mrs. Cametta said, munching on a corn muffin. Sibella was thankful Maureen and the two Charlies were still asleep, because it gave her mother a chance to sympathize with her. "Diaries are never safe from sisters," Mrs. Cametta said. "It was a rotten thing for her to do."

"Well, she's a rotten girl," Sibella pointed out.

"It's just that she's so jealous of your academic achievements," Mrs. Cametta went on. "Someday when you're older, you'll probably give your sister a medal when you realize how far she's gone on pure looks. Your poor sister was so slow in school, the teachers used to ask me if she was pulling a full train. I can't even give her a twenty-dollar bill and send her to the store. Some sailor would cajole it away from her and send her home with a lot worse than magic beans."

"It's like she hates me for something *deeper*," Sibella said.

"You can thank your father for that," her mother jumped in. "He thought he could just walk out and it wasn't going to hurt anyone except me. You seemed to understand, but Maureen's never forgiven him. I think whenever she does do something mean to you, it's because a part of her does hate you for going easy on your father. She still thinks he's a cockroach."

"He's not a cockroach," Sibella insisted.

"No, dear," Mrs. Cametta agreed. "That floozy he lives with who lets smoke curl up her nose and then back out of her mouth—*that's* a cockroach."

Sibella decided to walk all the way down to Richmond Terrace and take the Number 1 bus to the St. George ferry house, timing it to miss most of the commuter traffic. Aboard the ferry she bought a pretzel, a French doughnut, and a cup of coffee, then sat on the top deck feeding the sea gulls. The boat went by the Statue of Liberty and Ellis Island and Governor's Island, then docked at South Ferry. She walked from South Ferry up to a Chock Full O'Nuts on Broadway. She picked up a couple of whole wheat doughnuts and a large coffee to go.

Sibella made it to the laboratory by ten-thirty, and took the elevator to the fifth floor—where she remembered exactly which door led to her favorite person in the world. She knew he would be preoccupied, probably wouldn't even notice the door opening. Most of all she knew he would love being surprised. Inside, she looked across the half dozen lab tables and labyrinthine tubes connected to retorts and distillation apparati. He was alone, busy with a titration, carefully watching the drops fall into a beaker to see when acid would become base.

"Daddy," Sibella called softly.

Her father looked up. "Sibella! How are you? Come on over. I'll be finished in a second."

"I don't want to interrupt."

"No, no, don't worry about it."

She watched him expertly guide the titration to its conclusion. He still looked exactly like he did in the big photograph on her bedstand. Kind loving eyes, distinguished—just a touch of gray in his hair. He was the one person she felt hadn't changed on her.

"Your mother called," he said, taking her into his arms and giving her a big hug and a kiss.

"I figured she would," she said, unwrapping his coffee and doughnuts. "I haven't see you since Thanksgiving, so I thought I'd just take a ride in."

"Ah, my favorite doughnuts." He beamed and then added, "Your mother sounds as spaced out as ever. She was telling me about her new boyfriend. How affectionate and considerate he is. But she seemed very disturbed about Maureen and what she's been doing to you—giving you a hard time as usual."

"Yes, Dad."

"There's a kit to build a computer I could get you. You could just make a code and keep your diary in that. Nobody would be able to pull it out or retrieve it except you. You look like you're feeling pretty good." He smoothed the hair on top of her head.

"Well, I am," Sibella admitted. "So I said this morning, to hell with school, I've got to go and see the wizard."

"I don't know how much of a wizard I am. But I've been meaning to tell you, I've got a secondhand binocular microscope for you for Christmas."

"Oh, Dad, you *didn't*!"

"Look, I said I would. I did. It's a honey. They were using it in the National Aniline Division on Rector Street—but they're phasing that lab out. Remember when I had you doing the experiments on supersaturated solutions and you ran up here with those flasks of copper sulfate? This is the same kind of scope."

She couldn't resist wrapping her arms around him.

"I miss you, Daddy."

"I miss you, too," he said. "But you're coming along fine, just fine. Please don't be too impatient. That's all I worry about. You're too smart, Sibella. I think you made yourself too smart just to make me happy, so maybe it's my fault, but I'm very proud of you, very proud."

"Daddy, I needed to ask you about something," she said gently, solemnly. She leaned her head against his shoulder.

"From what I hear, you're going to ask me something about love."

"Right on the nose, Daddy. You taught me about atoms and condensers, foot candles and electrodes. I know Ohm's law and horsepower

96

and the corpuscular theory—but I don't know anything about *love*."

"Why don't you tell me about this boy? Your mother said he worked at some kind of midget racetrack. Tell me about him. Is he special?"

"Daddy, I feel like I'm going to die if I don't have him. I want to *own* him. I want to pick him up in my arms and go running down the street with him and tuck him into my tool kit," Sibella said desperately. "I love him so much I wish we could *explode* together. That our atoms and electrons could get *inside* each other. I'm so sad. I love him so much, I'm sad, that's how special he is."

"Did you tell him this?" her father asked very seriously.

"Yes."

"Well," her father said, "then you've given your heart away."

Sibella lifted her head from his shoulder. She looked into his eyes to find out whether that meant she had done right or wrong.

"I used to give my heart away," her father said. "Not to Pauline," he clarified, evoking in Sibella the memory of her dad's girl friend. "I gave it to your mother, and you know what she did with it. I think it's very good to give your heart away a few times at your age, just so you know what dazzling love can be like; but then you learn that there are laws of science. I can only really tell you what you will learn to do eventually, and this law I call the law of love's *reciprocity*. It means you don't give your heart to anyone unless you know he wants it, and wants to give you his."

"How can you know this?" Sibella asked, listening to every word as though he truly was a wizard.

"Well, you see there's a lot of pieces to the human body and soul besides the heart. When you learn to practice the law well, the next time you see a boy you think you could love very deeply, you first say Hello. You start very small and see if there is any response. If the boy says Hello back, then perhaps you offer him a piece of candy. If he takes the candy, then you wait, perhaps days, weeks. And if the boy is interested, *if he's going to be the right boy for you*, he's going to offer you something, perhaps a piece of cake. And then one day you might offer him your hand, or even a kiss, or say, 'I've got some tickets to a good horror flick'—and if he takes that hand or that kiss or that movie then you wait again. Give him a chance to measure out some act that will signal you that he values you in equal weight. No matter how short or how long it all takes, finally the day comes when you'll know it's time to give him your heart. And when you do, be absolutely certain you want him to give you his. You'll know when he's ready. And when you accept his full love, then there is just one final rule I have to give you. That rule is *Don't then turn into the same kind of pain in the ass your mother did.* This world is teeming with men and women who have won the hearts of their lovers and don't know what the hell to do with them."

"Dad," Sibella whispered, understanding every word he had told her, "I think I'll be able to do that *next* time, but what do I do *now*? I feel so crazy. Daddy, I want to do something crazy. I love this boy so much and he's very freaked out. He's lost. He couldn't offer me a stick of bubble gum, much less his hand. This boy is going down the tubes. There are so many heavy trips lying on his head, I feel as though the entire world has let him down. Daddy, I want to do something *crazy* to make it up to him. I want to do something so nuts that I think maybe he'll believe again. I want to give him a chance. Am I crazy to want to give him a chance?"

Her father looked at her thoughtfully, again smoothing her hair with his hand.

"This all comes under the category of *desperate acts*," her father said with a little laugh. "The only rules I would say you should follow now are two: *One*, don't hurt anybody; and *two*, don't get knocked up. Anything else I think most of the world would consider as just a part of growing up, and I don't want to interfere with any of that. I knew from the moment I held you in the nursery, all eight pounds, seven ounces of you—I said, 'This is a special girl. This is a sexy, little, brilliant girl, and she's going to have one of the most spectacular lives of any girl in the world.' You're always going to be original, Sibella. And some people will call that crazy. I find it daring, beautiful, and you are the most cherished invention I have ever made. Do your something crazy. *Shock* a few people. I trust you, Sibella. I've always trusted you, and believed in you."

Sibella lifted her lips and gave her father a big,

solid kiss. "Oh, God, you're a sweetheart. You're one big, one-hundred-percent-pure sweetheart." And then she laughed, singing, "Crazy, crazy, here I come!..."

13

Sibella got home just after noon. She was glad the house was empty—a rather recurrent gratitude. She got her bankbooks. By one o'clock she was at the Chase Manhattan Bank on Forest Avenue. By two o'clock she had finished at Citibank and was at Del Amor Dodge. By four o'clock the salesman had driven her straight off the lot in the Surfer van. He had insisted on showing her every detail of the van. He said it was the first time in years anybody had walked in with that much cash, even for a used van. He showed her the V-8, the power steering, and the overhead console as though he himself had crafted them. He was thrilled with the bay window, carpets, and paneling, and with the rear gaucho bed. He was so thrilled, she could hardly turn him off. In fact, the only way she could shut him up was when he tried to tell her how to get maximum performance and she said she was already planning on blocking the manifold heat riser in order to divert heat away from the air-fuel mixture. She said she had several steps in order to end up with a cooler, denser mixture that would contain more power-producing oxygen. That's when he shut up entirely and followed her instructions to drive his licenseless customer to Innis Street and park under the approach to the Bayonne Bridge. The van Dan had stolen for the joyride was gone, so she knew it had to be back at the Wing Brothers lot.

"You sure you don't mind walking back?" Sibella asked him.

"No," he said, his eyes still glowing with excitement. From the moment he had seen her packages of hundred-dollar bills, he had begun literally to shake with anticipation.

"Good luck," he said. *"Good luck."*

Sibella walked to Dan's apartment, knocked on the door a dozen times—but he wasn't there. She went across to the midget raceway. Inside, the passageway to the garage was almost empty, and she could see the garage was dark. A couple of hundred kids were mobbing the pinball machines, so she had to push her way past the counter and twin blondes. Louie was out on the track as the official dispatcher. She went to the counter and spoke to one of the girls.

"Is Dan around?"

"He doesn't work here anymore," she was told. "But I saw him hanging around—I think he's playing the machines."

The sight of the machine area was especially freaky and active with flashing lights. The bells and beeps and sound recordings were deafening. *He could be right in front of me and I wouldn't know it,* she thought, the noise was so disconcerting to her mind. She'd have to focus in closely. She moved to a Captain Fantastic machine, pretended to be playing it. One replay for 88,000 points. She let her eyes glance over the entire wall. There was the Faces pinball machine, and the Time 2000 pinball machine that invited her to experience the "Future of Pinball." There was the Six Million Dollar Man—he was yelling, "Red alert! Full bionic power!" and some jerk was lit up with a cartoon caption saying, "Good luck on your mission." And then there was the Playboy machine with young and old ladies nude, frolicking around in hot tubs and waving to electronic men. There was the Spirit of '76, which had a lot of different electronic tracks, and on the far wall were the Sundance machine and the Speed Freak, the Seawolf, the Drag Race, the Midway's 280 ZZZAP. Right behind her was the Digger Gremlin, a color maze, and another machine that promised she could ambush the Asteroid M70. There were the laser guns and the Astro Fighter, and the Love Tester where for a quarter she could find out if she measured Blah, Clammy, Mild, Wild, Sexy, or Hot Stuff in the sex-appeal department. But most of them were war machines, where for a quarter anyone could take control of the Missile Command, or the Star Hawk. There were the Big Vendor machine and Tank! and Middle Earth, and flashing roaring Cosmic Gorilla, the Galaxian with its electronic screams, the Stunt Cycle, a mechanical arm wrestler, the Indy 800, the Tailgunner, the Chase, the Space Marauders, the Fire Truck, and there, in the middle of all the machines she saw—

DAN! He was firing a light gun past little plastic bears that would throw up their arms and die whenever the electrophoto cell in their shoulder got hit. He looked so pathetic. She wanted to cry. He looked like all the rest of the kids, taking their hatred and disappointment out on all these horrendous games. There were the Mrs. Fitzgeralds and the Louies of the world, sticking their little keys in the backs of the machines and emptying out all the kids' money. It was horrible people that stuck these machines in there, that invented these machines. They designed these mechanical bandits to fleece money out of the young. Big old bosses preying upon kids. She recalled very clearly the vision of Mrs. Fitzgerald closing her wings around Dan at the Drop Inn bar, fluttering, drinking like a pert selfish vampire bat.

"Hi, Dan," she said. He looked at her like he was really stoned. Either that or so deeply depressed he couldn't even react.

"I've got something to show you," she continued as he turned his attention back to the gun. He let off a barrage of shots, connecting with three bears that let out painful growls and threw their arms up into the air before keeling over.

His face looked longer, thinner. It was gaunt. His hair hung more limply than usual. She knew he needed her very much. It was true he didn't look exactly like he was in a teenage magazine at the moment. He didn't look like anyone could run a caption along the bottom of him, "What makes him soooooooooo lovable?" They couldn't print up a story that his long heavenly hair was exactly the kind a girl would like to run her fingers through. And his body wasn't "foxy" at the moment, and there was no "sexy smile" that was adding up to "a hunk and a half." They couldn't do a couple of paragraphs about his personality. They couldn't say, *Oh, Dan is kind of shy, but once he gets to know you better and trusts you, he's your friend for life. Our wonderful playboy of the month is tough and macho with the guys, but warm and tender when he's around the girls. He's soooooooo very athletic and just loves rock and roll, and can talk about his fave groups for hours.* No, those magazines were published and written by more old vampire bats.

This was just a boy who needed her.

She took his hand. "I have a surprise," she said. "Just trust me, *trust* me."

"It's cold out there," he said.

"Then button up." Before he could complain any more she had him out the door.

"Why are you looking at me so *funny*?" he wanted to know.

"I just can't wait to see what you think about my little surprise."

"What?"

"If I told you, then it wouldn't be a surprise. You're just not going to believe it, not going to believe it at all."

She dragged him across the street and down the block to the spot where Innis Street went under the Bayonne Bridge approach.

"This is dumb, Cametta," he said.

"Just keep your eyes on the bridge," she ordered. "Keep looking up until I tell you."

"You're nuts. You're freaked out and nuts," he said.

Sibella stopped. She put her arm around Dan and pointed. "There it is," she said. "Now you can look." She leaned forward—she didn't want to miss a single reaction on his face when he saw the Dodge Surfer van.

"I still don't see what you're..." His voice trailed off, his eyes were glued straight ahead of him. He was looking at the van. She waited. She saw his mouth open, his jaw drop a full inch. She was waiting for the smile, for the cry of joy as it would sink into his head that she had bought the van for *him.* She took the keys out of her pocket and waved them in front of him. "It's *yours,*" she said. "It's a present from me to you."

Still she waited for his reaction.

"What did you *do*?" he said, finally, too softly.

"I bought if for you. I took out all my savings. It's yours. I paid cash."

"I don't understand."

"*Merry Christmas!*" She gave him a big squeeze and rested her head against his shoulder.

"I can't believe you did this," he finally said. "I don't understand."

"There's nothing for you to understand," she insisted.

Now he was looking at her, eyes opened wide. *"What do you mean there is nothing to understand? Who the hell do you think you are, Sibella Cametta?! Just who the hell do you think you are?"*

"Dan, I..."

"You think you're going to *buy* me? You think you bought me with that Dodge van? You think that's how cheap I am?!"

"I thought you'd . . ."

"Get away from me!" He began to shake her off. "Get away from me, you *lunatic*!" He turned and started moving swiftly back toward the Mariner's Harbor Midget Raceway.

"But it's your *dream*," Sibella cried out, running after him. "You said it was your *dream*."

He kept walking, faster. "I should have known you were a sicko. You're *bananas*, girl! You're like a mutt, just running around sucking after me. If you tell me one more time how I'm your big prince with a great destiny ahead of me, all the great big things waiting for me in this life . . . Well, you're a *freak! You're nuts! You make me want to throw up right in the snow.*

"Dan I only wanted to . . ."

"Do you want to know what I really think of you?" he asked, stopping short, his voice vaporizing, coughing like a steam locomotive. "You're a joke! You think nobody sees you when you come snooping around me? They *see* you. I *see* you. And you know what everybody says about you? They say a lot because you stand out like a big clown. Everybody laughs at you! *I* laugh at you! You're a walking, *ugly little joke*! I tried to be nice to you, but you made my stock go down! Whenever I see you, I feel ashamed. Don't you dare tell me I'm such a winner. *I don't like losers telling me anything!*"

He crashed his way up the steps to the main

building toward the pinball machines. She stood frozen in the snow watching the door close behind him. She stood several minutes unable to move; finally she turned and somehow managed to walk home.

14

On Sunday she was finally able to write in her diary again. *Dear Diary, I haven't seen him since Friday. I haven't been able to think or read, or write. Now I've got to tell someone, so I'll tell you, even though I know my sister will probably find this and read it on the radio, or in Times Square or someplace. Anyone who reads this deserves to find out what it feels like to have your heart broken. I wake up in the middle of the night with a pain in my heart. My body has turned very, very cold, and I am in terribly agony. I feel as though I have died in silence. I feel despair. Loneliness is a very sad affair. All my hopes have burned out. He's taken all of me with him. Thare is no one really left inside me. There will never be anyone for me to share my life with. I can't hide the hurt inside, and I'm not even asking for any pity. Pity is a big bore. And if I ever tell anyone what really happened, they'll say I was out of my mind anyway. I tried walking along the street yesterday, but wherever I go my heartbreak follows. Everywhere I turn, he is not there. I played the game for the first time, and I played it wrong. It is Christmas Eve. The loneliness is now unbearable. Everything is so mixed up and I can't stop crying. My mother keeps asking what's wrong, and I tell her nothing. I know she knows I've lost him. She brought me a cup of tea and cookies, and I know she wants to help me, but she can't. There isn't any point in living anymore. Maureen begged me to let her help me, but I know she's just got a guilty conscience. I wish I was not on earth anymore. I wish I was dead. I am dead. I thought about killing myself, perhaps jumping from the bridge, but I'm too sad to even do that. I thought about calling Bertram. I thought about buying love from some boy who could be bought. I've tried to even come up with a hypothesis of how to come out of this, but I can't. My science has failed me. I can't fix this with a hammer and a nail.*

By seven that night she was already in bed. The lights were out but she couldn't sleep. She lay on her back, staring up into the darkness. Her blood felt like it had an overdose of caffeine and chocolate. She lay there for what seemed like hours. At first she thought it was a dream, even a nightmare, the buzzing sounds, the muffled voices. She heard her mother saying, "Too late, too late. Oh, it's too late. You can come back tomorrow. And then in this dream she heard a voice yelling *"Sibella! Sibella!"*

She came to full consciousness and still heard the voice. It was Dan calling from downstairs, *"Sibella!"* She heard her mother protesting; even Charlie began raising his voice. She flew out of bed, yanked open the door, and hung over the railing. "I'll be right down," Sibella yelled.

"It's too late," Mrs. Cametta called up.

Sibella saw the picture from her high-angle point

110

of view: Mrs. Cametta red faced. Charlie ready to sock this poor boy with all the snow in his hair.

"It's *not* too late," Sibella insisted. *"Wait there, Dan. I'll be right there!"*

Sibella dashed around like a mouse. There were so many parts of her body to worry about. Her teeth—she'd brush her teeth. It was cold, she had to wear enough clothes, maybe gargle. Her hair, she'd put a cap on to hide it. The fake fur! She was so tired of wearing the fake fur, but it was so warm. She'd wear her brown-suede leather boots. So what if the snow ruined them! By the time she got downstairs everything seemed to be smoothed over. Mrs. Cametta and Charlie, even Maureen and Chucky, seemed to have realized that this young boy intruder might turn out to be the best Christmas present that house could get. It took them only one look at Sibella to see her face flush with hope.

"Don't be too late," Mrs. Cametta said.

"I won't," Sibella promised.

She took Dan's arm and got him out of there fast. Out on the front porch she almost tripped over his suitcase.

"I got kicked out of my apartment," Dan explained.

"What did they do that for?"

"They wanted me to pay rent," he said, "But it doesn't matter. I'm on my way to Florida.

"I've been looking for you for two days, you know," he said.

"How did you find me?"

"I asked the guy in Steckman's. He told me

where you lived and said you did a great job on the fluorescent lights. He showed me one of the Formica countertops you helped him with, too. It was a pretty good job. And when he said Treadwell Avenue, I remembered you saying that was where you lived."

Now he reached out and took her arm, helping her over a stretch of ice. But in the cold of the night she began to feel very, very depressed again, even though he was at her side. She didn't know what to say as the snow fluttered down on them and they both began to shiver

"I thought we'd get a beer," he said. "You could have a hot cocoa."

"We could go to the van," Sibella said softly. "I don't think I could stand anything like the Drop Inn."

"You didn't take the van back?"

"Nope."

"Where is it?"

"Under the bridge where I left it," she said.

Dan reached into his jacket, pulled out a little package of Kleenex, and blew his nose as they headed into Innis Street. "I know I was *horrible*," he said. "I don't know what happened to me. I just freaked out. I was rotten, Cametta. I was really rotten, a screw-up—*Dan Screw-Up*. That's what they ought to call me, 'Dan the Big Royal Screw-Up.' I'm sorry, Cametta. You're the only one who's ever really rooted for me. Nobody roots for me. They all jump up and down on me. Nobody would think about giving me a Hershey bar, much less a Dodge Surfer van. I think I just blew up because I didn't know how to deal with it any other way."

"You *were* horrible to me," Sibella said, her eyes focused on the icy pavement, her voice almost freezing in mid-sentence.

"Oh, yeah, I just said that," Dan admitted. "But it wasn't meant as an invitation for you to go on a prolonged bummer. It's gross enough that this is Christmas Eve without you sinking us even further down. I thought you'd be glad to see me," he said, putting his arm around her shoulder now.

"Well," Sibella stated, "knowing you got kicked out of your apartment and you're leaving for Florida doesn't exactly make it an evening of zest for me."

"Hey, *look*," he said, dropping his arm off her, "you think I found you because I'm hard up? Man, I could be at twenty parties. They fired me from the racetrack, but let me tell you they still liked me. Janice wanted me to go with them, and a lot of other people over there. There's going to be a big party at Shoal's, and I was invited to a lot of homes, too. I could have been by a hearth singing Christmas carols. This one girl who always played the Montezuma's Revenge pinball machine—you may have seen her in there the other night, the big blond one, with globes like basketballs—she had me all set up for a classy party. You're not talking to some hard-up kid, I'll tell you that." He kicked a chunk of ice and watched it skid ahead, then he put his arm back around her. "I guess I just thought of *you*," he said more calmly. "I guess I felt as though I wanted to *apologize* to you."

"Why are you going to Florida?"

"Well, I've got zilch here. I've got a friend down there who works on a yacht at a marina in Fort Lauderdale. I knew him at McKee Vo-Tech. He sent me a picture one time of him grinning picking an orange off a tree. I figure I'll look him up. See, I'm the kind of guy, if I'm not freezing to death, I'll get along. I could sell roses on street corners, clean fish, and I'm one of the best bus-boys you ever saw. I'll make some money, and then maybe go into something like supplying staff uniforms for a hotel or something. I'm not stupid."

When they got to the van, she gave him the keys. He opened the door on the driver's side and helped her slide across. He started the engine. Soon the first vapors of heat began to drift from the vents. The streetlight shots rays through the snow crystals on the windshield, and pieces of ice began to warm and slide downward like the walls of a melting ice palace.

"Why did you buy the van?" Dan said. "I just don't understand why you did it. I won't be able to leave until I know that."

"Because I *believed* in you," Sibella answered. "Granted I was madly in love with you, and thought you were the answer to every dream I ever had. But I think I mainly did it to give you a chance."

"You spent thousands of dollars to give me a chance? You spent enough money for the two of us to go on an African safari, or live in Bombay for a year.

"*I still want you to have the van.*"

"Why? I still don't understand why."

"Because you told me it was *your* dream. So at least one of us got their dream. And I really don't care what you do with it. I know you're leaving, so just get in it, and you can drive off and do whatever you said you were going to do with it. And there's *no strings*. You don't have to hold me. You don't have to kiss me. You don't have to even say goodbye. I think I've got a lot more chances coming up than *you* think *you* have." She sighed deeply. "Dan, I've never given anything to anybody before, not really."

"I can't take the van."

"Sure you can. If you want to do something for me, you can send me a key chain. I like key chains. Maybe you'll find one that has a little souvenir of Fort Lauderdale on it. Or someday maybe you'll find a seashell. If you're walking on the beach sometime and you see a seashell, and if you want to, send it to me. That's what I'd really like."

"You are nuts, aren't you?"

Sibella looked away, tears coming into her eyes.

"*Do you still love me?*" he wanted to know. "Do you still think I'm your dream boy come true? Isn't there just a little part of you that's hoping I'm going to take you and smother you with kisses and hug you to death, spend the whole night with you in the van? And I'm not saying that to be mean. I'm just being practical. I'm just trying to

115

tell you that if that's what you'd like, I wouldn't mind doing it. I've done it with a lot worse than you." He reached down and took her hand. She tried to yank it away. "You're not *my* dream come true," he said. "But I like you. I would *enjoy* kissing you."

"Maybe we just better stick to the seashell," Sibella suggested.

She still couldn't look at him, but she felt him lifting her hand. He had moved it next to his face. He placed his lips against her hand. For a moment she thought music was beginning to reach her mind from a very far place. Then she realized he had simultaneously turned on the radio. He was moving. She could hear he was doing something, but she closed her eyes. Now he was behind her, pulling her hand. She slid slowly backward toward him—and opened her eyes. Now they were sitting on a rug in the back of the van where the stained-glass bay windows made it seem as though they were in a church. He took her face in his hands, turning her gently until she had to look directly into his eyes. He was looking at her in a way she had never seen anyone look at her. It was as though a spell had taken over. His eyes were glazed. He pulled her closer, his mouth dropping slightly open. Words were gone. There was only warm magnetism, a magnetism drenching his entire body. What was even more startling to her was that she felt her own thoughts slowing, words stopping somewhere between her ears and fading. She knew what was happening to her would never find its way into her diary. This was something for which there would never need to be a reminder, nor a witness. What was happening was beyond her dreams, her hopes, her family, school, and even her tool kit. This was a law greater than physics or chemistry. Greater than death. As his lips touched hers, she knew why she had been born. The last picture in her mind before she fell so totally into his body was that of a great proud lion, a shouting ringmaster. And then came the prancing white horses as the circus came to town.

By midnight Sibella stood on the one snowless spot under the Bayonne Bridge. Dan and the van had gone. Finally she was able to walk. She found herself alone walking farther down Innis Street, then turning onto Morningstar Road. In just a few minutes she was at the bridge plaza with the cold mechanical sounds of the toll booths mixed with the sloshing of car tires cutting into salted snow. She went up the stairway to the start of the pedestrian walk. There was a phone booth. She stuck in a dime and dialed.

"Hi, Mom," she said.

"Sibella, where are you?" her mother wanted to know. "I can hardly hear you. Sibella, where are you? It's so late."

"I'm at the Bayonne Bridge, Mom."

There was a long pause. Sibella could hear her mother's mind making an adjustment, even changing her breathing.

"He's gone to Florida, Mom. He's left for Florida. He's *gone*."

"Sibella," Mrs. Cametta said slowly, measuredly, "I'm sending Charlie in the car to get you. You just wait right there." Sibella heard her mother shout to Charlie. She heard the apprehension in her voice. She missed one or two of the muffled remarks because her mother had her hand clasped over the receiver tightly. In a moment she was back. "Sibella," Mrs. Cametta said, "you know you were just *physically* in love with him, don't you?"

"I don't know what I think."

"Sibella, I need to talk to you. I want to tell you I'm sorry we haven't talked more. *I think you needed something I didn't give you.* What your father told you was right. Sibella, are you there?"

"Yes, Mom."

"Sibella, I was only *in* love with your father, that's why it didn't work out. You're only *in* love with this boy. It's very strong and it's very terrible to have so much to give. I'm not saying it's this boy's fault any more than it was your father's fault. This is just something that happens at your age. Sibella, you won't walk out on the bridge? *Promise me you won't walk out on the bridge.*"

"He's gone," Sibella said again, now barely able to form the words. "He's gone and I'm very cold."

"Sibella." Her mother now began to sound terribly worried. "Charlie is going to be there in a moment. Sibella, I know you think Charlie is a jerk, but with him and me there is loving. That's what you really want, Sibella. Loving is when someone does things for you, too. You're going to learn about that. When a boy starts to worry about you, and wants to do nice things for you. When he wants to help *you* with your homework, or bring *you* a flower or a new pair of pliers. When a boy calls *you* and asks how *you're* feeling. Sibella, are you there?"

"I have to hang up, Mom," Sibella said. She heard her mother's now-frantic voice come out of the receiver, but she replaced it on the hook. Now she was alone again.

As she walked along the footpath out onto the bridge, she watched the houses grow smaller and smaller, and the river come closer and closer. When she was over the shoreline, she stopped and looked down from the railing. The cars looked the size of matchboxes flying along Richmond Terrace. Just to her left and out in the middle of the kill a great oil barge was floating toward the sea. *Oh, my God*, she told herself, *I'm going to kill myself. Something has gone crazy in my head and I'm going to fall and die. I can't control myself. No one ever told me this is what happens, this is why people kill themselves. They all made it sound like suicides choose to kill themselves, but I'm not choosing. There's something out of control. It's not me making me die. It's something deep inside of me making me grab this railing. . . .*

The touch of the cold metal pulled her consciousness back into better control. *How horrible loving someone is*, she thought. *What a vicious trick of Nature.* Now she leaned her head down onto the cold railing. She placed her forehead against it, then her cheeks. She grabbed a piece of icicle and rubbed it on her neck. The coldness was keeping her in reality. She mustn't lose that reality again or she could straddle the railing in a moment and be over the edge. She was one motion from

119

falling hundreds of feet and destroying herself on the concrete below. A bad voice inside her told her she shouldn't move out farther onto the bridge. If she fell farther out, she might only hit water. She might live. A tug might suddenly appear and whisk her out before the freezing waters could freeze her. No, the cement of Richmond Terrace was safer, *deadlier.* Here was the spot to die.

"I trust you, Sibella. I've always trusted you, and believed in you." She heard her father's voice now. It seemed to be coming from a part of her every bit as deep as the bad voice. If her father so trusted her, so believed in her—what on earth could it be in her worth trusting? She wasn't special. She had heard stories about a lot of girls who wanted to kill themselves over boys. Even tonight, on Christmas Eve, she knew the suicide rate was higher than ever all across the country. She imagined hundreds—no, *thousands!*—of girls just like her lined up on bridges or on ledges of windows. Hordes of lonely girls who had lost their boys, or had never found one, opening bottles of pills and getting the nooses and razor blades ready. *Ha! Sibella Cametta, the great scientist! Sibella, the great believer in the Laws of the Universe, and Nature! Sibella, who loves Nature, who believes that in all of science there is design and meaning and purpose. What meaning can there be in the deadly, overwhelming feelings of a girl who wanted a boy?*

A church bell began to toll, then another. St. Roch's bell tower was sounding just off to the north. Now Dickenson Methodist and the Harbor

120

Baptist. . . *It's midnight!* she realized. *Santa Claus coming. All the presents. Children asleep and dreaming. It's the holidays! The time of holidays*—and she kept her face pressed to the cold railing, "I trust you, Sibella," her father's voice came again. *And if you trust me*, Sibella answered her father in her mind, *then you must trust me to figure my way out. You believe in me to figure my way out of love. You believe in me to recover. . . .*

I must recover, she started to tell herself. *How can I possibly recover?* She began to fight the bad voice inside. She would fight it with small measurements of hope, even though at that moment she didn't believe in hope. *Someone will be nice to me. Maybe that's where my mind has to start. Maybe it will be a teacher at school who will say a nice word that isn't too preposterous. Maybe a boy will hold a door for me. Maybe someone will lend me their umbrella. That's a possibility. I have to fix my heart. I'll get out a different set of tools. I'll stick myself under the binocular microscope. I'll look at my faults and grow up a little. Just a little. Maybe I can do that. Maybe I can picture myself slightly happy again somewhere. Maybe I can blossom just a bit in time. I should let myself have a lot of time. I should believe in Time. Maybe I can find myself for the first time in my life. Maybe I can like myself. Maybe this is what my father believed I could do. I could find myself and start feeling good about myself and flowers and spring and rain and cats and dogs and parameciums and even boys again. I could spend my days in creative ways. I have so many things I know how to do. I could wait for love, be more patient for love. I could watch television and be nice to friends and bake chocolate chip cookies and build a whirligig. I could slowly get over old memories, get over the shame and pain at having thrown myself at Dan. . . .*

She paused at the thought of his name. It was still very strong. She could share her feelings with her mother and Maureen—and even their Charlies. And she could believe that even she herself would find love one day. Maybe it wouldn't be easy, but she would find it. The days could get brighter, and one day she could even find room in her heart to remember Dan and not the pain. One day she could think of him and really hope he was okay wherever he was. Yes, all of that could be. If only she could have the answer to one last thing: *Why did God or Nature or whoever it was give such powerful feelings to any young girl? To me? To all young girls! Why?* And she knew very well she was asking for the secret of Love.

The church bells were amplified in her head, deafening now. The stars shone like sparklers. Great magnesium-white dots! Suddenly a chill ran through her body and she lifted her face. The chill was one of joy. It was the special tingling excitement she always had when an answer was becoming clear. It was the chill of solving an equation. The exhilaration of the last nail driven into a bookcase. It was the perfect tuning of a spark plug, and the last brush of a fresh coat of paint. Her head became a complete circus as she realized she almost had the complete answer. In her mind she saw her father and mother together, still talking. She saw Maureen desperately flying through her universe of boys, clutching, *grafted* onto Chucky. She saw herself and all the Charlies of the world and even Mr. and Mrs. Brightenbach, caring, worrying about batteries, billions of lovers buttering English muffins and making breakfast. Her thoughts were coming too fast now as the bells lifted her higher and higher. Her mind was encompassing all of humanity, all that Love was *supposed to do.* This aching, bursting, exploding, hurting, burning—this maddening feeling in her heart *had* to be that strong. Only something that powerful, that consuming and *passionate*, could hold a boy and a girl together for the long, long time it would take for a marriage, for a child and children, for happiness and a caring even through divorce and death. Love *had* to be strong enough to last a lifetime, and strong enough again for still *another* lifetime if that was needed.

She moved away from the railing, back to the roadway of the bridge. *And I'm only fifteen*, she told herself as the headlights from passing cars ignited in her eyes. Soon the car would come that would take her home.

ABOUT THE AUTHOR

PAUL ZINDEL is the author of eight novels for young adults, a picture book, four theater plays, and numerous screenplays. He has an M.S. in education and has received an honorary doctorate from Wagner College. For ten years he was a high school chemistry teacher on his native Staten Island, New York, and then was awarded a Ford Foundation grant as writer-in-residence at Nina Vance's Alley Theater in Houston, Texas.

He enjoys television, movies, dream interpretation, swimming, and all fattening foods—particularly Hunan cuisine and ice cream. He also likes new experiences (he's currently trying his hand at acting) and teenagers who need someone to confide in.